HOT JOCKS 5

DOWN
AND DIRTY

New York Times & USA Today Bestselling Author

KENDALL RYAN

Down and Dirty
Copyright © 2020 Kendall Ryan

Developmental Editing by Rachel Brookes
Copy Editing by Pam Berehulke
Cover Design and Formatting by Uplifting Author
Services

This book is a work of fiction. Names, characters,
places, and incidents are either the product of the
author's imagination or are used fictitiously.

ABOUT THE BOOK

From New York Times bestseller Kendall Ryan comes a delicious new standalone romance featuring an accidental Vegas wedding and a totally perfect alpha hero.

Remember that time you accidentally woke up in Vegas married to your hot younger guy friend?

That's basically my life right now.

Mistakes we made, okay?

He's too young for me. Twenty three to my thirty.

And he's saving himself for the right girl.

Yup. Apparently I've married the last alpha-male virgin on the planet. And my stubborn, oddly traditional, new husband doesn't want a divorce.

He wants *me*.

Complicated doesn't even begin to cover it.

PLAYLIST

"Freqing Out" by Chris Domingo, Mariner, featuring Alec Sky

"Doin' It" by LL Cool J

"La Femme d'Argent" by Air

"A Girl Like You" by Edwyn Collins

"Feel So Good" by Mase

"In the Meantime" by Spacehog

"Soul Meets Body" by Death Cab for Cutie

"Tonight, Tonight" by Smashing Pumpkins

CHAPTER ONE

Cheers

Landon

"**B**uck up, soldier," my friend Owen, star goalie for the Seattle Ice Hawks, says as he thumps one hand on my shoulder.

Easy for him to say. He's engaged to the woman he loves, and is loved by adoring fans across the country. Basically, he's got the world by the balls.

In comparison, my life feels like it's on the brink of falling apart. But no one wants to hear me complain about that right now, because we all just flew in by private jet to celebrate Owen and Becca's joint bachelor/bachelorette party in Sin City.

Yay.

Cue the sarcasm.

"I'm fine," I say, tipping my chin toward the

packed dance floor. "Go dance with your soon-to-be wife and quit bugging me."

Owen's gaze strays over to where his fiancée, Becca, is on the dance floor, moving her hips beside a couple of our female friends, one of them being Aubree Derrick. Aubree, the petite brunette with the killer curves and fiery attitude who captured my attention the second I met her. She's a total smoke show. But I try not to let myself notice things like that about her, because the minute I do, I need to go on boner patrol.

My drink arrives as Aubree dances, or rather shimmies her ass in one direction and flails her arms in another. As I watch, I laugh for the first time all night, because dancing is *clearly* not her strong suit. But she's still hot as fuck, and I can't take my eyes off her.

The club is loud, almost deafening. Deep, sultry bass thumps around me, and the room is dim except for the flashing blue and purple lights. It's been easy to go unnoticed, tucked inside the curved booth while the rest of our group makes good use of the dance floor.

I take a sip of the stiff drink in front of me, hoping it will calm some of the pent-up energy stewing inside me. From the outside, my life seems great

. . . I'm a twenty-three-year-old rookie on one of the best hockey teams in the country, earning close to seven figures. But I didn't get much ice time this season, and now I'm not sure where I stand with the team.

My future feels like it's on the brink of collapsing, and all I can picture is having to move back home to live with my dad, and get a minimum-wage job at the shoe store I worked at in high school, while some other asshole is living my dream. I signed an entry-level contract, which means there are no guarantees. Next year could be it for me. If I don't get more playing time, why the hell would Coach keep me? I'm an overpriced bench warmer. A bearded cheerleader.

I rub one hand across my stubbled jaw, remembering that I shaved a few days ago. Scratch that— I'm a sulky cheerleader minus the beard.

A few seconds later, the gorgeous Aubree slides into the booth next to me, and I scoot over to give her more space. "Why aren't you dancing?" she asks, bringing the straw in her vodka soda to her lips to take a long drink.

Her pulse thrums steadily in her neck. She's flushed and slightly breathless. My gaze strays to her lips before I can look away.

I shrug. "Don't really feel like it."

"You don't have to babysit tonight, Covington. You can get drunk and make bad decisions along with the rest of us." She smirks, watching me closely as she leans in and sucks on her straw again.

She's referring to the fact that I usually abstain from drinking, happy to play the role of designated driver when the team goes out.

"This isn't water," I say, swirling the clear tequila in my glass, lifting a brow in her direction.

"Good." She pulls a tube of lip gloss from her purse and runs it over her lips. Seriously, is she trying to taunt me? "For the record, I never thought that was fair that they made you play DD as the rookie on the team."

I turn and glance at her. *God*, she's like a cookie I want to bite into. "They didn't make me. I choose not to drink during the season."

"Oh." Her mouth parts in surprise, and her eyes twinkle. "So you mean to say that you guarded our drinks while we danced, drove people home, and even humored drunken requests for burritos at all hours because of the kindness in your heart?"

I chuckle. "Something like that."

"You're one of the good guys, aren't you, Covey?" She pats me on the thigh with one slender hand, and my groin tightens.

Aubree and I met for the first time earlier this year at a charity event. As the director of the team's charity organization, she's friendly with most of the players and their girlfriends, and has been a frequent member of this new crew I've found myself pulled into. But she's never once expressed any interest in me. Never looked at me like I'm anything more than just the rookie on the team.

I've told myself it's a good thing—that I don't have time for distractions this season. But now she's giving me a hungry, desire-filled look, and I'm weak as fuck.

Aubree slowly pulls her hand away and adjusts the spaghetti strap of her little black dress, calling attention to her cleavage.

I shift in my seat, trying to alleviate the sudden pressure I'm experiencing below my belt. "I mean, I pay my taxes on time and I haven't murdered anyone, but let's not get carried away."

She laughs, amusement dancing in her honey-colored eyes. "You are. I can tell."

I don't disagree with her. Sure, I'd like to think I'm a decent human being, but let's be real. Being a good guy doesn't get you very far.

Exhibit A is the current state of my life. Single as fuck and horny—which isn't exactly a winning combination, even though I've brought it on myself. Being celibate is a choice, but that doesn't make it any easier. And when you throw in my fears about getting canned from the team, let's just say I'm not exactly a barrel of laughs tonight.

Aubree makes a pensive sound and watches me over the rim of her glass like I'm a puzzle she wants to solve.

My self-imposed abstinence isn't usually a problem, and while I'm not picky, I am selective. And the gorgeous girl beside me makes me feel a little unsteady. Like she's capable of pushing past all my inner defenses without even trying.

Am I out of my element? *Yes.* Does that only make me want to push harder, strive for more, and take more chances? *Bingo.*

When Aubree lets out a lengthy sigh, I glance at her. "Everything okay over there?"

I expect her to say something mundane is bothering her—like maybe those insanely high heels she's wearing—but it seems Aubree is full of surprises.

"Ugh . . . where to start." She fiddles with her straw again. "Let's see. I'm thirty and single, which is basically like the kiss of death." She meets my eyes quickly before deciding that's too intimate and scans the dance floor again. "All the good guys my age are already spoken for."

She's never opened up to me like this before, but something inside me appreciates her vulnerability. I turn to face her and meet her eyes. "You're a ten, so you could have any guy you want. Your dancing skills are questionable, but still."

"You're an ass." She rolls her eyes, but the tint on her cheeks at hearing me call her a ten is evident.

"Not denying that."

She smirks and stirs the ice cubes in her drink with the straw.

"Cheers to being single." I raise my glass to hers, and Aubree clinks her near-empty cocktail to mine. "Should we order another round?"

"God, yes. Immediately."

Her timing is perfect, because our cocktail

waitress has seemingly appeared out of nowhere, and we quickly place an order for another round of drinks.

It's over our third cocktail that Aubree blurts, "So, who here is your type?" She sweeps her arm around the bar. "I'll help you pick someone out."

My sip of tequila goes down the wrong pipe, and I cough to clear my throat.

Is that what Aubree plans on doing tonight? Picking out someone tall, dark, and temporary to provide some stress relief? More importantly, why does the idea of that bother the hell out of me?

"I don't have a type," I finally manage to say, my throat tight.

Aubree scoffs. "Everyone has a type."

"Are we seriously doing this?" My tone hints at annoyance, but in truth, I'm anything but. Sitting here talking and laughing with her is the most fun I've had tonight. To be honest, it's the most fun I've had in a long time.

"What about her?" Ignoring my question, she nods toward a blonde swaying her hips on the edge of the dance floor. She's dressed in a barely there halter top and a tiny black leather skirt.

Frowning, I shake my head. "No."

Aubree turns and glares at me. "What's wrong with her?"

It's strange how expressive she is. I study her for longer than I should, unable to tear my gaze away. But rather than answer her question, I plead the fifth with a shrug and take another long gulp to drain the rest of my glass.

"So, are you going to tell me your type, or what?" Her eyes fix on mine and stay there for what feels like too long.

I don't hate it.

"Fine. I prefer brunettes."

She smiles triumphantly. "There. Was that so hard?"

Trust me, I'm halfway there, sweetheart.

Quizzing me while she sips her beverage, Aubree gets me to admit that I like petite brunettes who can hold a conversation and are feisty.

She quirks one eyebrow in my direction, and I'm suddenly certain that she's just realized I'm describing her. Thankfully, she doesn't call me on it. She just continues tapping her finger against her chin, scanning the bar for prospects like an athletic scout does at a training camp.

"There's got to be more than that," she says, challenging me. "Breast man? A nice heinie? What's your thing?"

"My *thing*?" I can't hide the humor in my voice. "First off, don't use the word heinie ever again."

"But—" she says.

God, I love that she's about to vehemently defend even *this*.

I hold up one hand, stopping her. "Promise me. Never again."

Aubree makes a low sound of agreement, and I feel a sudden ache in my balls. "Just answer the question, lover boy."

"Tits are nice," I say.

Aubree laughs, the sound deep and throaty, and any regrets I had about muttering *that* inarticulate phrase vanish. I'd do it all again just for a shot at hearing that laugh.

"But a nice curvy ass is pretty great too. I'm a guy, so I wouldn't deny either."

"Truer words," she says with a chuckle.

I'm about to turn the question around on her, ask about her type, but the words stick in my throat. I don't want to hear her describe any man here who isn't me. My ego isn't secure enough for that tonight. Sad but true.

Aubree's got perfect tits and a nice curvy heinie—*God, that word really is atrocious*—and I can't *not* make a play for her. At this point, what do I have to lose?

"You want to get out of here?" I ask, adjusting my watch, feigning a casual posture.

Her lips twitch with a smile. "And go where?"

I shrug, trying to play it cool, but my heart is hammering. "Anywhere. Someplace we can talk."

She considers this, weighing my offer as those expressive amber eyes flash on mine again. "Talking is good."

So is kissing.

"Sure," she says at last.

I settle our tab and rise to my feet, grateful that the night is taking an unexpected turn.

CHAPTER TWO

Mistakes Were Made

Aubree

The rays of sunlight shining through the hotel curtains feel like a flashlight shining directly in my eyeballs. No, not a flashlight. Laser beams. A hundred laser beams, all pointed directly into my corneas.

Hell hath no fury like a hangover when you're thirty years old.

With an exhausted groan, I roll to the edge of the bed, feeling around the side table for my phone, which kindly informs me that it's almost eleven in the morning. *Jeez*. If it were any other Saturday, I'd already be home from yoga and hopping in the shower by now.

But I'm not at home in Seattle, I'm in Las Vegas, and at the moment, just the thought of yoga makes my stomach turn. The only downward dog I'll be doing today will be directly over the toilet. That is, if I can force myself out of bed.

Last night, I was throwing back vodka sodas like I was still twenty-one, back when hangovers were a mythical thing that only happened to *real* adults who just couldn't keep up.

Let the record show that I, Aubree Derrick, can't keep up. My head is pounding, and there's a churning in my stomach that I'm not even sure throwing up would fix. So, yeah, those real adults? I guess I'm officially one of them.

Since I'm not particularly excited about the idea of leaving this bed, I open my texts, looking for clues as to what exactly went down last night. By some miracle, I find no evidence of drunk texting any exes. Or if I did, my drunk self had the wherewithal to delete the evidence so Sober Me didn't have to be embarrassed. *Thank you, Drunk Self, for being a true friend.*

But I'm not in the clear yet. I still need to check my camera roll.

I tap the icon with my thumb, holding my breath as I swipe through photos of me and the girls, Owen and Becca posing at dinner, and a goofy selfie Elise must have snapped when I wasn't paying attention. I'll be sure to save that as ammo for a future birthday post for her. But that's it.

A slow, relieved breath leaves my lungs. Thank the good Lord above, because other than the hangover from hell, I actually got away scot-free.

Until I hear the rustling of sheets coming from the other side of the bed.

Oh no. I spoke too soon.

Slowly sucking in a deep breath, I count down from ten, promising myself that by the time I reach one, I'll have worked up enough courage to face whoever I brought back to my hotel room last night.

Three.

Two.

Two and a half.

Two and a quarter.

One.

At first, I don't recognize the mess of dark hair and tanned skin lying next to me. My bedmate is facing away from me, giving me a delicious view of his muscular back. Faint red lines run down the sculpted muscles between his shoulders, definitely the work of my fingernails.

Wait a second. I know that back. It's one I'm used to seeing draped in a jersey.

Number 94, a.k.a. Landon freaking Covington, the Ice Hawks rookie, is asleep in my bed. Shirtless. And although the sheets are pulled above his trim waist, the pile of clothes on the floor is a pretty good indication that he's naked below the waist too.

It doesn't take a detective to tell you what that means. *Shit got real last night.* My heart takes off like a race car, thumping so loudly that I'm sure it's going to wake him up.

Okay, Aubree. Deep breaths. It's a hookup. People do this all the time. It's no biggie.

And then I catch a glimpse of my left hand. Staring back at me is a beautiful halo-cut ring with a huge diamond that is most definitely a biggie. Literally and figuratively.

My gaze pings between my left hand and the sexy man sleeping next to me, trying to fill in the gaps in my memory. Slowly, it starts coming back to me—the feel of his strong arms wrapped around me, him whispering something in my ear that made me laugh like a hyena. Us stumbling down the Vegas strip together, hand in hand.

But after that, things start to get a little foggy between midnight and now, when there's a naked man in my bed and an enormous diamond ring on my left hand. You do the math.

I peel back the covers and tiptoe as softly as humanly possible to grab a sleep shirt from my suitcase. I don't need Landon waking up to the sight of me wearing only a thong, scouring the room for proof that we used a condom last night.

But that's exactly what I do.

I check the trash cans for a torn silver wrapper, a mysterious bundle of toilet paper, anything to give me peace of mind that we used protection last night. But no. The only remnants of our drunken evening together are our clothes, lying in heaps on the floor, and a certificate from Happily Ever After Chapel that I spot on the dresser.

With quivering fingers, I hold it up, scanning the fine print for something that says this is just a souvenir we picked up. Instead, I find the scrawled signatures of our witnesses and the cold hard truth. Landon Covington and Aubree Derrick are certifiably joined in wedlock.

Panic rises, tightening my throat and squeezing my chest until I can hardly breathe. It's like my lungs can't expand all the way, and my heart is beating so fast, I think it might explode.

I'm not sure if the sound I make qualifies as a shout, a sob, or somewhere in between, but whatever it is, it wakes Landon up. He jolts upright in bed, fumbling for the sheet to keep his lower half covered.

"Holy shit, Bree. Are you okay?"

My mouth opens to reply, but no words come out. Just shaky breaths and a throaty moaning sound as I drop the marriage certificate, letting it float to the carpet. I can feel my cheeks go pale as the blood rushes out of my face, and I crumple onto the edge of the bed, resting my head in my hands. Shallow, uneven breaths push past my lips, and I feel so light-headed, I could faint.

"Fuck." The bed shifts as Landon scrambles out of it, tugs on some article of clothing from the floor—pants, I think—and rushes to my side. "You're okay, Aubree. Take a breath."

He strokes my back until I'm brave enough to pull my face from my hands and look him in the eye, which only gets my heart racing again.

"You're doing great. Can you breathe with me?" He inhales through his nose, urging me to do the same, then releases the air slowly through pursed lips.

As I come down from my panic, he keeps his arms tight around me like a security blanket, holding me flush against his chest until my heart rate slows to match his. A few minutes of deep breathing later, I'm in enough of a normal state to pose the question demanding to be asked.

"Did we . . ." I fumble for the right words, gesturing to the sparkling rock on my finger. "Is this real? Did we get married?"

He nods slowly, pushing a strand of hair out of my eyes and tucking it behind my ear. "Yes, to both. The ring is real and, according to that piece of paper you were holding, the marriage is too."

"I . . . I don't remember any of it," I whisper, dropping my gaze to my feet.

"Really? I didn't know you were that drunk. You seemed pretty with it last night."

"Well, I wasn't," I mumble. "If I were *with it*, I would've suggested we use a condom."

Landon flinches. "Hold on. What?"

I repeat myself, drawing out the words. "A condom. We should have used one."

But this time, instead of a look of confusion, he looks back at me with a smirk. "You really don't remember anything, do you?"

"No!" I huff, folding my arms over my chest. "Can you please clue me in?"

"We didn't have sex," he says, his voice equal parts blunt and soothing.

My brow crinkles as I try to read his expression for signs of sarcasm. "Are . . . are you sure?"

"I wouldn't lie about that."

"But what about the marks on your back?" When Landon's face twists in confusion, I gesture toward the mirror. "See for yourself."

He pushes off the bed and stalks toward the mirror, his eyebrows lifting as he gets a look at his back, sizing up the marks running from his shoulder blades to the small of his back. "I guess you got a little rough when we were making out."

Rough? Me?

Maybe I was really into it?

Slowly, the fog covering my memory starts to

lift . . .

· · ·

We were outside the door to my room, laughing and kissing while I dug through my purse for my room key. Landon shushed me playfully, pressing kiss after kiss into my neck until I finally got the door open, making a big fuss of hanging the DO NOT DISTURB sign on the handle.

The second it clicked closed behind us, our mouths collided, his tongue greedily exploring mine as my hand cupped the bulge growing behind his zipper. He moaned into my mouth, a deep, lustful sound that triggered something primal inside me that I couldn't quite explain. His hands moved up my thighs, slipping under my dress to touch the front of my panties, and he groaned when he felt the damp fabric. I leaned into his touch, my knees parting to accommodate his fingers.

"C'mon, Mrs. Covington," he growled into my ear. "Let's take this to bed."

And we did, falling into the center of the huge king-size bed together.

Fumbling with the buttons on his dress shirt, Landon finally got it off. His chest was broad and smooth with wide pecs, and I stroked the firm muscles, unable to stop touching him. When I reached his abs—dear God, they were amazing—I made a happy sound, and Landon chuckled.

Panting, I said, "God bless hockey players."

"Amen." His lips moved against my throat.

My dress was rucked up around my waist, and his eyes darkened with hunger as he looked at the scrap of black lace between my legs.

"Damn, you're sexy," he murmured, trailing one large palm over my hip, sending little sparks of heat racing down my spine.

While he leaned closer, kissing my neck, I arched into him and trailed my hand down his back, enjoying the feel of warm, sculpted muscle beneath my fingertips.

With one more sweet kiss, he pulled back so he was kneeling between my parted thighs. I worked my dress off over my head, which was no small feat. Landon groaned at the sight of me, his gaze locked on my bare breasts.

"Jesus, Aubree." His voice was little more than a harsh pant.

He tested the weight of my breast in his hand,

his thumb skating across my nipple, and I sucked in a shaky breath.

"I really like these," he murmured.

"Yeah?" I could hardly get the word out, I was breathing so hard.

"So much."

He watched me with a dark, hooded stare, seeming unsure, like he was hesitating. But I knew he wanted me, as evidenced by the enormous erection tenting the front of his dress pants.

I worked my hand under his waistband and ran my palm along his impressive length. *Wow. There's a lot of him.* His eyes sank closed and his mouth dropped open as he moved his hips, seeking more friction against my palm. *Holy hell, that's hot.*

His face was flushed, and when he opened his eyes, they were bluer than I'd ever seen them.

He expelled a breath, and his pelvis lifted.

"Holy fucking—" He didn't finish, just groaned loudly as my palm wrapped around him.

• • •

And then the memory fades.

I blink at the softer, sleepier-looking version of Landon sitting on the bed beside me. His hair is a mess. It's kind of adorable, if I were in a state to notice such things, anyway.

"I sort of remember that," I say, blinking the memory away as I reemerge into reality. "But I could use some clearing up on what happened after we made it to the bed."

"Well, we kissed," he says, his voice steady but measured.

"I remember the kissing."

He nods. "And you took off your dress."

I draw in a breath, feeling my face turn warm at the memory of shoving my hand in the front of his underwear. "And then?"

"And then?" His thumb touches his bottom lip. "Then you, um, fell asleep. So I covered you up and placed a glass of water on the nightstand for you."

Landon's expression is calm, his tone matter-of-fact. I have no idea why he's not freaking the heck out right now like I am.

My gaze wanders to the full glass of water still on the nightstand. "You're shockingly casual about this whole thing, you know that?" I hurl the accusation at him, my frustration rising.

He shrugs. When he runs a hand along the stubble at his jaw, I notice something else.

"Why don't you have a ring?"

He looks down at his naked left hand, his brows pushed together as though he's working to recall the hazy details. "When I bought your ring, we looked at some for me too, but you said you'd get mine after your next payday."

"Oh." My stomach plummets. "Sorry about that." Even my drunk self knew that my nonprofit salary couldn't accommodate an unplanned wedding ring. And definitely not on the same paycheck that paid for this Vegas trip.

"Don't be sorry. I offered to pay for both rings, but you insisted. It was kinda . . . sweet."

I do my best to smile, but it comes off more as a grimace.

What's so sweet about a drunken Vegas marriage you can hardly remember? And why is he so cavalier about this whole thing?

Before I can formulate a question, the sound of both of our phones buzzing in unison drags me away. It's a group text to both of us from Becca.

```
Good morning, lovebirds! Come
down to breakfast in the lob-
by! We've got two seats call-
ing your name. <3
```

"I guess we should get ready." I sigh, tossing my phone onto the duvet with a huff. "We're wanted at the breakfast table."

Landon tugs on last night's clothes to make the trip down the hall to his own room.

Meanwhile, I barely make it through my shower routine without throwing up. Between the nausea, the headache, and the life-altering decisions I made last night, it looks like vodka and I won't be seeing each other for quite some time.

Landon must take his sweet time getting ready, because even with the time it takes for me to dry my hair and put on half a face of makeup to conceal the dark circles under my eyes, we still arrive at the elevator at the same time. *Great.* Looks like the newlyweds will be walking into breakfast together.

"You look nice," he says, nodding toward my navy-blue T-shirt dress.

"No need to flatter me," I remind him, biting

my cheek to maintain my composure. "We're already married, remember?"

Landon's expression is unreadable, except for the slight tic in his jaw. I wish I knew how to read him better, because I have no idea what he's thinking.

When the elevator doors open on the ground level, it doesn't take long for us to find our friends. Mostly because the second they spot us, the whole table starts whooping and whistling about the newlyweds. A drop of nervous sweat slides down my spine. This is going to be worse than I thought.

Justin, the hockey team's star center, who's normally pretty reserved, is the first to jump to his feet, leading a dramatic slow clap as we walk up to the table. "Look who decided to show up. The mister and missus!"

I slide into a seat next to my friend Bailey, hiding my red cheeks with a menu, but Landon doesn't make it that far. Teddy, one of the team veterans, slaps him on the back, and Owen, the team's fun-loving goalie, pulls him into a side hug that quickly becomes a headlock.

"Covey's officially off the market, ladies!" Owen says with a laugh.

Once he breaks free, Landon chooses the seat directly across from me and pours two glasses of water from the pitcher on the table, then slides the first one to me. I accept it with trembling fingers.

"So, how does it feel to wake up a married man, *Lovey*?" Elise asks, a wicked glimmer in her eye.

"It feels like I'm hung over as fuck." Landon snickers, and the whole table breaks into laughter.

Well, the whole table except for me. I must have steam coming out of my ears or something, because after taking a bit more teasing from the guys, Landon leans across the table, his brilliant blue eyes brimming with concern.

"Are you okay?"

"No, I'm not fucking okay," I whisper back. "Why would I be even a little okay with this?"

"Oooh," Owen hollers from across the table. "Are the newlyweds having their first lovers' quarrel already?"

My throat constricts. *Shit*. I need to get some air before I start crying in front of all my friends.

"Excuse me," I whisper, swallowing the lump in my throat as I push back from the table. I'll pick up fast food or order room service later or something. But I can't sit and take any more jokes about the dumbest mistake of my life. Especially not while I'm feeling like total shit.

"Hey, hey, wait up," a voice calls from behind me, and before I can make it out the revolving door, Landon catches me by the arm, his long, calloused fingers curling around my wrist. "What's wrong?"

I spin to face him. His eyes are now a dangerous shade of blue. A shocking, brilliant blue that makes me feel a little weak as I pull a breath into my lungs.

"I'm glad your teammates are so amused by our situation," I manage to say through gritted teeth. "Because I sure as hell am not."

"Come on, Aubree. They're just joking around." He reaches for my hand again, but I pull it out of his reach.

"It's not a joke. It's my *life*. And once I have a functioning, non-alcohol-poisoned brain again, I'll be getting legal advice from Sara, and we're going to look into how to get this annulled."

Landon's eyes meet mine, his gaze determined. "Just take a breath."

I do, releasing it slowly as my heart pounds.

"Last night was a mistake," I whisper, looking down at my sandals.

"Maybe. Maybe not." He swallows the words.

When I look up again, he's staring directly at me, his face expressionless.

I breathe out a shaky breath. He can't be serious. "Okay, I thought I was the one with a nonfunctioning brain. You saw that certificate, right? That was a real ceremony. We're *legally* husband and wife right now."

"I know we are," he says, his voice strained. "Which is why I'm taking this seriously."

My mouth falls open and I blink at him, dumbfounded, waiting for him to laugh and tell me he's joking. Or, better yet, that this whole thing is one big prank, that the ring and the certificate are fake, and this is some elaborate joke that he and the rest of the group concocted.

But when he stares back at me, the look of determination in his eyes sends a shiver trampling down my spine. All I can do is laugh in disbelief. It was either laugh, or sob loudly.

"Landon, if you're suggesting that we stay married . . ." I pause, trying not to scoff at the thought while giving him another second to say *gotcha*. But he doesn't. "Well, then you're even more immature than I thought."

His face falls for a second, then steels into a stern expression, his angular jaw ticking in a way I can't quite read. "We'll talk about it later. This weekend isn't about us; it's about Owen and Becca."

I make an aggravated sound. "Then why is everyone talking about *us* instead of Becca and Owen?"

Since when is there an us?

He closes his eyes briefly, and I watch his Adam's apple bob as he swallows whatever emotion he's choosing not to show. "I'll handle it. Just come back to the table. You'll be in a better mood once you have some coffee."

My eyes narrow at him, but he doesn't back down.

"And possibly some eggs," he adds, and I straighten my shoulders.

"I don't like eggs." When he frowns at me, I say, "Make it pancakes, and you have a deal."

"Done and done. Pancakes on me."

I follow him back into the restaurant like a runaway puppy returning home with its tail between its legs.

"Aw, did we kiss and make up?" Becca coos, riling the table up again.

"Enough." Landon's barked order, coupled with his dagger-sharp look, quiets everyone down, at least long enough for us to place our orders.

After that, every time I look up, Landon is staring at me. His scrutiny makes my stomach tighten in a way I haven't felt before.

When our food arrives, the conversation dies down as people dig in. Once we start talking again, the subject switches to Becca and Owen's honeymoon in Greece.

"Everyone always raves about Mykonos, but Santorini is really more our style," Becca says, squeezing her fiancé's hand as he chomps down on a piece of bacon. "Right, O?"

Owen shrugs. "As long as I have my angel by my side, I don't care where we go. We could go to freaking Cleveland, for all I care."

"We are *not* going to Cleveland," Becca says sternly, giving him a pointed look.

Owen just chuckles and steals a piece of bacon from Becca's plate while she smiles at him like he hung the moon.

I snicker along with the rest of the table, and Owen takes my smile as a free pass to sneak back into dangerous territory. A devilish look comes over his face as he folds his hands on the table, faking the most serious expression he can manage.

"So, Covey and Aubree. Where are you two going for your honeymoon?"

Before I can even process my anger, Landon has the situation under control. "Guys, can we let my wife eat her pancakes without any more comments, please?"

The table goes quiet again. Although it's a little awkward, I can't say my throbbing headache and I really mind the silence.

What I do mind is the fact that Landon just called me his wife. But I'll deal with that later. With a hangover like this, you take your wins where you can get them.

CHAPTER THREE

Honeymoon for One

Landon

My drunken friends' encouragement last night was one thing—but Teddy changing my regular room for the honeymoon suite while I'm in the hotel gym? That's on a whole other level.

You're welcome, is his text reply to the message I send the guys on my team when my room key no longer works.

I spent the entire last year getting pranks pulled on me—it came with the territory as a rookie—so there's no reason to assume that my keycard has suddenly demagnetized or something as benign as that. I know my rowdy-ass teammates are to blame.

WTF? I text back, sweaty and standing in the hall, and he replies,

Go to room 2001. 20th floor.

Cursing under my breath, I take the elevator up from the ninth floor to the twentieth, and discover that room 2001 is the honeymoon suite. The irony isn't lost on me. An envelope taped to the door is labeled LOVEY, the nickname they bestowed upon me during the first team skate.

A room key is tucked inside the envelope, which I use and then shoulder my way through the double doors. My suitcase is already there, parked beside a heavy mahogany table in the foyer.

The room is massive, and it certainly can't have been cheap, but Teddy signed a four-year extension last year worth $12 million. He can afford to waste his money on extravagant splurges, but I can't. Which is why when I found a crumpled receipt in my pocket during brunch from a luxury jewelry store—for a $30,000 three-carat oval-cut diamond set in a double-halo platinum band—I almost fell out of my chair. The ring on Aubree's finger is stunning, there's no denying that. But still.

With a defeated sigh, I head into the marble bathroom and strip out of my sweaty gym clothes. Cranking the faucet to hot inside the massive glass shower, I step under the rain-head fixture and close my eyes, but not before noticing you could easily fit another four bodies in this shower. Not that my night will involve anything is exciting as that.

After my shower, I explore the rest of the suite with a towel knotted around my waist. It's an impressive space, but somehow that only makes me feel worse. It's not the type of room you should have all to yourself. I grab a pair of black boxer briefs, relieved that the guys didn't fuck with my suitcase.

One time on the road for a game in Montreal, they broke into my hotel room and stole all my underwear. I was forced to show up commando for the morning skate, where I paid one of the PAs a hundred bucks to run out to the store for me to buy more. Shaking my head at the memory, I grab a clean white T-shirt and a pair of black gym shorts.

There's a living room with a velvet teal-colored sectional. It's modern and low to the ground, one of those things that looks good but won't be comfortable to actually sit on. A round glass coffee table is in front of it, facing a massive flat-screen TV mounted on the wall.

I bypass the living area and head for the bedroom, with its massive king-size bed dressed in white linens. Collapsing in the center of it, I read through the group text thread from my idiot friends.

Owen and Becca are heading to a nice steakhouse for a date night, and a few of the others are talking about getting tickets to see a comedy show. I notice Aubree hasn't chimed in. I was clearheaded enough at breakfast to ask for her number, which I didn't previously have. I'm almost surprised she didn't put up more of a fight. She didn't exactly seem pleased with me this morning. But a man needs his wife's digits—this is a universal truth.

Another universal truth? A dude should never spend the night after his wedding alone in a honeymoon suite. This shit is depressing as fuck. I turn on the TV mounted across from the bed to distract me, but it doesn't. In the back of my head, I can't help but draw some rather somber comparisons.

All my life, I've prioritized sports over romantic relationships, telling myself it was the wise thing to do. Only, now I have to wonder. Am I destined to end up lonely and alone, just like my dad? It's a sobering thought, one that doesn't sit well with me.

My father has married and then divorced four times. Maybe it's in my genes, and I'm destined to wind up just like him—with a string of bad decisions, a trail of broken relationships, alone and lonely with no one and nothing to show for it. I guess the apple didn't fall far from the tree.

Perhaps it's stubborn male pride, or maybe it's foolish optimism. I really have no idea what makes me decide to text Aubree. Hell, maybe it's my competitive spirit, but whatever the reason, I type out a greeting.

`Hello, wife.`

It gets the desired reaction. She texts me back immediately.

`OMG. Don't call me that!`

`So, funny story . . . TK had my room switched to the honeymoon suite.`

`Is this all just some big joke to you?` she fires back quickly.

My hand tightens around the phone as I type out a reply. `Not at all.`

I haven't seen her since that disastrous brunch this morning, and she's not participating in the group chat, so I have no idea what her plans are for this evening. Hell, she could have flown back to Seattle early for all I know. Said *fuck it* to this entire weekend, wanting to get as far away from our nuptials as possible.

Hoping for the best, I reply.

```
What are you doing tonight?
```

Her response comes a few seconds later.

```
Just staying in. I don't feel
like going out.
```

```
Same. Do you want to do nothing
                    together?
```

There's a pause, and I clutch my phone a little tighter while I wait. I'm pretty sure she's going to shoot me down, and I'm not sure why the idea of that bothers me so much.

```
I don't know if that's the best
idea.
```

```
Yeah, but this suite is incred-
ible, and it's on TK's credit
card. The least you can do is
help me get even by running up
the mini-bar and room service
charges. The bastard deserves
                            it.
```

Fine. But I'm wearing my pjs.

Perfect. Room 2001. See you soon.

When I hear a soft knock on the door ten minutes later, I don't expect the tightness I feel in my chest. With a deep breath, I head over to answer the door.

True to her word, Aubree is wearing pink-and-gray striped pajama pants and an oversize T-shirt that says in block letters SORRY I'M LATE, I DIDN'T WANT TO COME. Her dark hair is in loose waves, and her amber eyes look anywhere but directly at mine.

I smirk, nodding toward her shirt. "Seems fitting."

She rolls her shoulders, feigning a smile. "I'm here, aren't I?"

As I watch her walk through the suite, pausing to pluck a bottle of water from the kitchenette, then stopping to admire the view out the floor-to-ceiling windows in the living room, memories of last night come crashing back to me in vivid detail . . .

When we left the club together, we wandered around the Vegas strip for a while, talking and laughing. We stopped briefly to watch the fountains dance in front of the Bellagio, and Aubree rested her head against my shoulder as we stood there. It was nice being there with her—just the two of us.

Afterward, we ducked into the opulent Sky Bar for another cocktail. The sour mood I'd felt earlier in the night had vanished because the girl beside me was fucking incredible. Later, we met back up with the group, where there was dancing and more shots.

Then things start to get a little hazy.

I remember arriving at the neon-pink-themed wedding chapel . . . going over the paperwork with our newly appointed wedding coordinator. Handing her my credit card. Aubree and I opted for the traditional wedding, not wanting some knock-off Elvis impersonator to officiate our vows. It was our first decision as a couple, and I remember being pleased we'd agreed on it together without hesitation.

I remember grinning like an idiot as Aubree walked toward me against the backdrop of traditional wedding music. Teddy was our witness, signing the marriage certificate at the bottom after the officiant. He was so into the whole idea—even calling in a favor to someone he knew who worked in the county clerk's office, getting them to issue us a marriage license in the middle of the night and drive it over. I have no idea how much that cost him, or why he and all of our friends were so encouraging. *Fuckers.*

It all took under ten minutes before Aubree and I were giggling through our "I do's" and then I was kissing her. Really kissing her. Our first kiss, which she returned with as much enthusiasm as if the whole thing had been real and two years in the making.

Afterward, we stumbled back to our hotel. I couldn't wait to be alone with her. We'd just done the most spontaneous, crazy thing, and all I could think about was continuing that kiss we started at the altar.

Now, as I stare at her, as inappropriate as it is, all I want to do is kiss her again. I'm pretty sure that's not going to happen, though, because Aubree is scowling at me.

Her gaze slips away from mine, and she gives the sofa the same suspicious look I did.

"The bed's more comfortable," I say.

She nods once. "Then lead the way."

I pause beside the bed as Aubree frowns. "What's wrong?"

"It's freezing in here," she says, looking at me like I should have known the answer to that question.

"Is it? Feels fine to me."

Wrapping her arms around herself, she marches over to the thermostat on the far wall and adjusts the temperature to her liking. Then she peels back the fluffy duvet and makes herself at home.

I pause, watching her.

"What? I always sleep on the left side," she says, tucking the blankets around herself. "Not that I'm sleeping here or anything."

"O . . . kay," I say. "Should I grab the room service menu?"

Aubree nods while reaching for the remote.

By the time I make it back to the room, she's changed the sports highlights show I was watching to some ghost-hunter documentary, complete with cheesy narration and poorly executed special effects.

"Here's the menu. Dinner starts on page six,

unless you want breakfast, which they apparently serve until eleven p.m."

She scrunches her nose. "I hate breakfast food."

"How can you hate breakfast?"

She shrugs, flips open the menu, and trails one slim finger along as she reads. I park myself at the end of the bed, watching her lips move as she reads. It's kind of endearing.

Seeing the ring on her finger is a shock to my system. I'm the one who put it there, with promises of a future on my lips.

Last night, I meant every word. Today, though? I feel more uncertain than ever—about everything, but mostly about my sanity. But I can't deny the strange bolt of satisfaction when I see the impressive diamond on her delicate finger.

"Do you want to talk about last night?" My voice is soft and a little strained.

"Nope. Not even a little bit," she says without bothering to look up.

I sigh, running one hand over the back of my neck.

Jesus Christ. Maybe it would have helped if

I had more experience in the female department. I've never even had a serious girlfriend, unless you count Tessa Hayworth my freshman year at Michigan, which I really don't. After six months of dating, she told me that she loved me, and I told her that I needed to focus more of my attention on hockey.

Spoiler alert: We broke up that day.

And now I'm supposed to know how to navigate having an insta-wife? Not fucking likely.

Hooking up with hockey groupies is the extent of my experience with women, but even those encounters I only let go so far before pulling the plug. I wouldn't let anything distract me from my goal. And yet here I am—in way the fuck over my head.

Last night, Aubree and I flirted and danced and kissed. Now, there's nothing but awkward silences and barely concealed hostility between us.

"Listen, things got kinda crazy last night, but that doesn't mean we didn't have a connection," I say, trying again. But Aubree continues looking down, her pink mouth moving as she silently reads the menu, or at least pretends to. "Say something," I order.

"Having a connection doesn't mean you should

marry the person after flirting for three hours." Her voice is tense, and a couple of awkward seconds of silence tick past before she meets my eyes and takes a fortifying breath. "We should just go back to being friends," she says almost sadly.

She wants to pretend last night never happened—go back to being friends?

As far as I'm concerned, our friendship was effectively ruined the moment I found out how good she tastes, and learned I loved the sound of her soft pants when I touched her. It's fucking crazy, but she's my wife, and for better or worse, I'm not ready to just let that go.

"Did you decide on dinner?" I ask, softening my tone and deciding to avoid the topic of her wanting to go back to being just friends.

"Would it be too much if I ordered both the filet mignon and the lobster fettuccine?" she asks, a smile teasing her lips for the first time tonight.

"Of course not. Better tack on dessert too."

"New York cheesecake or—*oh*, chocolate lava cake with caramel ice cream."

"Both."

Aubree's smile widens. "Excellent idea."

I pick up the phone and place our order, tacking on a $300 bottle of wine as one last fuck-you-very-much to Teddy.

As I stand at the edge of the bed, wrapping up the call, I feel Aubree's gaze lingering on my torso. The fitted T-shirt I'm wearing stretches taut across my chest, and the sleeves hug my biceps. My shorts hang loose on my hips, but the definition of muscle in my thighs is undeniable. When her gaze wanders up to mine, I lift one eyebrow and Aubree blushes, quickly looking away.

I toss the phone onto the foot of the bed. "Do you want anything from the mini-bar? I'm going to grab a beer."

"Ginger ale, if they have it. If not, lemonade."

After getting our drinks, I pause in the doorway watching her and can't help the inappropriate thoughts that skate through my brain. My wife is spectacular to look at. Trim waist. Small but perky breasts. But if I'm honest, I really enjoy her mouth. Lush and fiery and smart.

She's propped up against the pillows stacked along the headboard, her eyes focused on the TV, but when I enter the room carrying her soft drink, her gaze swings to me.

"Oh, thank you," she says, reaching for the can of ginger ale.

I settle in next to her and twist the cap off my beer. "Cheers."

"To?" she asks.

"To us, I suppose."

Aubree's eyes widen, and she pauses with her drink halfway to her lips. I can practically feel the panic rolling off her in waves.

"We don't have to decide anything tonight, okay? Let's just enjoy our dinner and this kickass suite."

"Okay," she says, her voice unsteady, her fingers curling tightly around the soda can.

She's fidgety and nervous around me. Why now? Last night was fun, nuptials aside. And the hot make-out session that followed was extra fun.

But right now, things are tense. And I'm guessing it's my job to make her more relaxed.

Shit. Well, here goes nothing.

CHAPTER FOUR

An Unexpected Development

Aubree

"**T**o us."

Landon's toast echoes in my ears like a gunshot. I blink down at the gorgeous ring on my finger, trying to absorb his words.

Something about him referring to himself and me as *us*, a single unit, stirs something inside me. It's been a long time since I've been in a relationship, but I never thought that my return to the dating world would cut straight to the end result. And now, staring at this ring, I feel the strangest mix of excitement and regret.

When I turn toward the man who gave it to me, I see that he's staring at the ring too. *Shit*. The poor guy is probably thinking about all the much better things he could have done with such a major chunk of his salary. And I work for the team's charity. What would people think if they saw me with such an expensive piece of jewelry? Probably that the money would have been better spent as a donation.

"So I've been thinking," I say, holding back a sigh. "You should take this back." I take one last look at the most beautiful ring I will ever see before shimmying it off my finger and holding it out to its rightful owner.

His thick, dark eyebrows pull together. "Why? Don't you like it?"

Even the suggestion makes me scoff. "Oh, come on. This is the kind of ring a girl dreams about."

Nodding, he meets my eyes with a sincere expression. "That's exactly what you said at the store."

"But you spent a fortune on it. And if we're not going to stay married, then there's not any—"

He holds up a hand, cutting me off. "I thought we agreed we weren't going to make any decisions about that tonight, so set that stuff aside. Forget about that and tell me straight out. Do you like the ring?"

I slip the ring back on, chewing thoughtfully on my lip as I gaze down at its brilliant sparkle. As I rotate my wrist, the light bounces off the enormous diamond, casting a spray of tiny rainbows around the room. Never in my life did I think I would get the chance to wear such a gorgeous piece of jewelry, not to mention own it. If not for the unusual circumstances, I'd be drooling over this thing.

"I love it," I finally admit on a whisper, my eyes still locked on the center stone. When my eyes meet Landon's again, his mouth quirks up, one dimple just barely visible.

"Then keep it. It's yours."

My lips part, ready to protest. Instead, I release a slow, staggered breath accompanied by a gentle fluttering in my chest. The feeling is unexpected, but welcome.

"Thank you," I finally manage to say.

"You're welcome."

As we sit here, our eyes locked on each other for a long, quiet moment, I take the opportunity to study Landon. Yes, he's an athlete, so his body is off-the-charts incredible, but his face is striking too. Bright blue eyes, high cheekbones, a square jaw. Dark tousled hair that's a bit too long on the top. Full, kissable lips that part slightly as he inhales, as though he's readying himself to say something.

But a knock on the door interrupts him, snapping us both back to reality.

"I've got it." He breaks eye contact, swinging one muscular leg over the side of the bed and stalking toward the door.

As he walks away, my gaze lingers a little longer than it should on his toned backside and broad shoulders. Can you blame me? Anyone with eyes can see that this man is drop-dead gorgeous.

But as much as I'm hesitant to admit it, there's more to him than that. There's something potent about him that my body reacts to on a basic level, which makes no sense because I don't know much about Landon. And what I do know leads me to believe we have little in common.

But the feeling that I get when I look at him, that warm, breathless feeling that makes my skin all tingly and makes naughty thoughts pop into my head, is undeniable. I literally just said we should go back to being friends, so why does the idea of waking up naked next to him again set my skin on fire? It's a question to ponder later, because Landon has turned around and is welcoming a tuxedoed man into the room.

"Hope you're hungry," he says, allowing the attendant to push the cart of food in before signing the check and sending him on his way.

"Wow. That's a lot of food. Where should we start?"

"I don't know about you, but I'm starting with that expensive-as-fuck wine." He disappears into the kitchenette and returns with a corkscrew and two stemless wineglasses. "Want some?"

I shake my head, then get to work removing our silver trays of food from the cart and laying them out on the bed. I already said I wasn't sleeping here tonight, which means getting crumbs on the sheets isn't my problem. When I finish setting up our meal, I slide back into bed to watch Landon try to wrestle the cork out of the sleek green bottle. The muscles in his huge forearms flex and jump, more entertaining than any show in Vegas tonight, I'm sure.

"I can't believe you're drinking again after last night," I murmur as he successfully frees the cork from the bottle.

"Hair of the dog, right?" He laughs, pouring

himself a glass.

I shake my head. Maybe that used to work for me back in college, but those days are long gone. When he slides back into bed next to me, I give his shoulder a gentle pat. "Talk to me again when you're thirty."

Annoyed, he grunts. "You're not that much older than me."

"Uh, yeah I am. Seven years," I remind him. "That's over a fourth of your entire lifetime so far."

He lifts a shoulder, unrolls a white cloth napkin containing a set of silverware, and hands it to me. "That didn't stop me from putting a ring on it, though."

I huff, accepting the napkin. "So much for not talking about it tonight."

"I said we weren't making any decisions," he says, correcting me as he uses a steak knife to cut into a piece of filet mignon. "I was just stating a fact. Our drunk selves could set our age difference aside. So, why can't we do the same while we're not drinking?"

"But you *are* drinking." I nod toward the glass of wine on his end table.

"A beer and a few sips of wine over the course of an hour? I'm not a lightweight. The point is, drunk or sober, the age difference doesn't bother me if it doesn't bother you."

I blink at him, struggling for one of my usual snappy comebacks, but I draw a complete blank. The only thought that keeps crossing my mind is how freaking gorgeous this man is. The last time I saw Landon in my bed, he was wearing nothing but the sheet. And trust me, I wouldn't mind having that view again.

But even in his fitted tee and athletic shorts, Landon looks totally gorgeous. Age aside, everything else about him is exactly what I'm attracted to in a man. From his boldly masculine physique to the five o'clock shadow dusting his chiseled jawline to his dark eyebrows and his large hands.

No. Stop looking at his hands.

I drag my gaze back to his to find him smirking. It's the first time tonight that I've been at a loss for words, and he's clearly counting it as a victory. *Ugh.* I can't decide if I want to kiss or slap that smug look right off his face. It's all very confusing.

"I'm too hungry to have this discussion," I blurt, twirling a fettuccine noodle around my fork.

When I look back up at him, though, he's grinning, unconvinced.

"Sure, Bree. Whatever you say."

The rest of the meal is spent in relative silence, apart from the sound of the ghost-hunter documentary on TV. We're both starving, and small talk would be a waste of time when we could be chewing.

Landon polishes off his entire steak in record time and has to help me with my filet mignon. These portions are insane, and I don't even finish half of my lobster fettuccine. By the time we reach dessert, the two pieces of cake staring at us feel more like a challenge than a reward. We opt to split the lava cake and save the cheesecake for later. Because there's always room for chocolate. *Duh.*

Reaching for a clean spoon, I do the honors of breaking into the perfect dome-shaped cake, sending the molten chocolate lava spilling out to mix with the half-melted caramel ice cream. One bite of that warm, chocolaty goodness makes my eyes flutter closed, and a low hum of satisfaction buzzes on my lips. I'm in heaven. Or at least I am until Landon pulls me back to earth, smirking into his fist.

My face falls, unamused, and my eyes shoot open. "What?"

"Nothing." He chuckles, his blue eyes twinkling with a devilish thought. "I just . . . remember that sound."

"What sound?"

"That sexy little hum. You made that sound for me a lot last night," he says, his voice low.

"I did not!"

I swat his thigh—which is, *whoa*, rock hard—then quickly turn my attention back to the cake. If I look in those sultry blue eyes another second, I'm going to blush. I just know it. And I don't want my pink cheeks giving me away.

"Sure, you can keep telling yourself that, but that won't make it true." He takes a hefty scoop of cake, smiling around his spoon. "Just like you can tell me you weren't checking my ass out earlier. But I'll still know that's a lie."

I nearly choke on my dessert in surprise. "What are you talking about?" I manage to say through a cough.

"You were sizing me up like a piece of meat at a butcher shop," he mutters, shaking his head, even though his expression is amused. "But it's all right. I like knowing you think I'm worth staring at."

"Shut your face," I say with an eye roll.

His smile only deepens, bringing out the dimple on the left side of his full mouth. "I have to ask. How'd I do?"

With a bored sigh, I huff out, "You passed, okay? Happy?"

"Extremely." He grins. "Now, finish off that last bite of cake before we get chocolate all over these fancy sheets."

I frown at the small remainder of cake up for grabs. "Um, no, that's yours. I had the first bite, so you should get the last."

He shakes his head. "No way. You're willingly spending our last night in Vegas with me in this ridiculous honeymoon suite. The least I can do is give you the last bite of cake."

I spoon up the final bite and hold it out to him expectantly. "It's not that big of a sacrifice, you know."

"I disagree. I think sacrificing the last bite of dessert is a very noble thing to do."

"Not that," I say with a laugh. "I mean spending the evening with you. It's not exactly a chore to sit here and eat expensive food in a fancy suite with a hot guy."

Landon lifts one brow. "So you think I'm hot?"

"I told you, you passed inspection," I remind him playfully, then lift the spoonful of cake to his lips again.

Giving in, he leans forward, parting his lips for the spoon while maintaining eye contact with me. It's strangely seductive. I can feel his low, rumbling hum buzzing through me as the chocolate hits his taste buds, his eyes sinking closed as he pulls back and chews, savoring the taste. The tingly feeling in my fingertips returns, but this time it's accompanied by a flash of heat that makes my heart race. I can't stop the sudden thought that I'd like to see him make that kind of delicious, low hum between my thighs.

"You, um . . ." I stammer, gesturing to my own mouth while looking at Landon's. "You've got some chocolate sauce right here."

His brow creases as one hand moves to his lips, wiping everywhere except where the offending chocolate is. "Where?"

"Right there . . . no, to the left . . . oh . . . may I?"

I know what I'm doing is dangerous, maybe even stupid, but I shift closer to him, sweeping my thumb over the chocolate on his lower lip.

"There," I whisper. "All better."

His blue eyes deepen to the color of a twilight sky, and the anticipation hanging in the air is borderline unbearable. His gaze flickers from my eyes to my mouth, and just when it's almost more than I can take, he grabs the hem of my T-shirt and gives it a firm tug.

"Get over here," he growls, and in one swift motion, his arms wrap around my waist and lift me into his lap.

The second his full lips crash into mine, I know all this small talk, this splitting of room service and arguing about age differences, has been a complete waste of time. This right here is what we should have been doing all night.

Our tongues flirt with each other, hesitant and careful. He tastes like red wine and bad decisions, and although I haven't had a sip of alcohol since last night, one taste of him and I feel instantly drunk. We move slowly at first, exploring each other for the first time without the interference of alcohol, but soon our pulses begin to race. And he becomes more reckless, kissing me deeper and deeper until he's devouring me with the hunger of a man who hasn't eaten in weeks.

The stiffness in his shorts presses against the juncture of my thighs, and I can't resist grinding against him, rolling my hips so I can feel his length through the cotton of my pajama pants. Shuddering at how good that feels, I grip his shoulders, digging my nails into his muscles, which makes him groan against my mouth. It's a huge turn-on to know I can get such a visceral reaction out of him.

The hand that isn't pressed against the small of my back floats to one breast and finds my stiff nipple, circling it until I give him a moan in return. The sensation is so all-consuming that I toss my head back, and he takes full advantage, running his lips down the column of my throat.

"You're fucking gorgeous." He groans the words into the curve of my neck, then trails his lips along my collarbone, leaving a trail of goose bumps behind.

"I want you, Landon," I whisper desperately against his ear, looping a thumb into his waistband. But as I tug, urging him to let his erection spring free, he pulls back, his twilight-blue eyes suddenly serious.

He shifts, inhaling deeply. "There's something I want to tell you first before we go any further."

Confused, I climb off of him, a lump building in my throat. "Is everything okay? Did I hurt you?" Maybe I was being too rough again.

"No, no. Not at all." He grins and nods toward the erection tenting his athletic shorts. "In case you hadn't noticed, I'm, uh, having a great time."

"Yeah, I kinda noticed."

Testing my luck, I reach out and give his impressive length a delicate stroke through his shorts. He inhales sharply, his eyes fluttering closed, but then his fingers wrap around my wrist, moving my hand away.

"There's something you should probably know first," he mutters. "It's not a big deal. Or maybe it is—hell, I don't know. It's just that I . . ."

When he pauses, my mind runs rampant with possibilities. Maybe it's something silly, like he has to run to the bathroom first. Or maybe it's something serious, like an STI. I hold my breath, waiting for him to finish his sentence.

"I haven't done that before."

I flinch. That definitely wasn't what I was expecting. I scan his eyes for signs of sarcasm but come up blank. Maybe I misheard him. "Done what?"

"I'm a virgin," he says, meeting my gaze.

I blink at him, the cogs in my head turning. "Like, a born-again virgin, right? There's no way you're an *actual* virgin." He's hot as fuck, *and* he's a pro athlete. That's just not possible, right?

A rosy color creeps up his angular jaw and across his cheeks.

Shit. Why the hell did I say that? I should have kept my mouth shut. His response says it all.

How stupid am I? I need to get out of here and put this poor man out of his misery.

"You know what? I'm sorry. It's late. I should probably get back to my room anyway." It's not much of an elegant exit line, but it's all I've got.

I scramble off the bed, tightening the drawstring on my pajama pants as I head for the door. My stomach twists as I bolt out, not even looking back when I rattle off a hurried, "Have a good night!"

Once the door clicks closed, I lean against it, trying to will my head to stop spinning.

Five minutes ago, I was making out with the hot-as-sin man who is legally my husband. And now I'm outside his room, trying to digest a piece of information about him that changes absolutely everything.

It feels like I just stumbled off a carnival ride. I'm hot and dizzy and confused. But I have a feeling this roller coaster ride is far from over.

• • •

Compared to the hungover hell that was Saturday morning, waking up on Sunday is a breeze.

No headache. No queasy stomach. No life-changing decisions made last night. I even managed to complete my entire skin-care routine before crawling into bed. *Go, me.*

All things considered, I should be feeling as fresh as a daisy. But here I am, using the hotel pillow to try to block the sunlight seeping through the curtains.

What should have been a good night's sleep was spent tossing and turning, thinking about what Landon shared with me last night and how poorly

I reacted. He was so vulnerable and honest, telling me something that, if I were to guess, even his teammates probably don't know. And what did I do? I ran away.

It seemed like a good idea at the time. I was, and am, floored that someone as dripping with sex appeal as Landon could be a card-carrying virgin. But I was too nervous about offending him to ask any of the questions piling up in my head. It seemed better to just leave.

But looking back, I know I could have handled it much better. I owe him a major apology.

I roll onto my side, trying to will myself awake, but the sight of the empty space in the bed next to me makes me want to crawl back under the covers and pretend none of this ever happened. But if I did, I'm sure I would just notice that my sheets still smell faintly of him, and that might make matters worse.

No more hiding, Aubree. You have to face the mess you've made.

Digging through the sheets, I find my cell phone buried in the bed, then scroll to Landon's contact, suck in a deep breath, and press the call button.

"Hello, you've reached Landon Covington

. . . ”

I hang up before I hear the rest.

Shit, straight to voice mail? Does he turn his phone off when he goes to bed? Looks like I'll be doing this the old-fashioned way.

Tossing back the covers, I sit up, grab the room phone off the end table, and punch the button for the front desk. "Hi, can you connect me with Landon Covington in suite 2001?"

The clicking of computer keys comes over the line, followed by an extended pause from the woman on the other end. "I'm sorry, ma'am, it looks like Mr. Covington has already checked out."

My stomach lurches. Where the hell did he go? It's barely nine in the morning, and our flight back to Seattle doesn't leave until four.

"May I ask how long ago he left?"

There are more typing sounds, followed by an answer that only leaves me even more confused. "A little over two hours ago."

Slowly, the pieces start to come together in my head. If Landon's been gone for two hours and his phone is going straight to voice mail, it's not turned off. It's on airplane mode.

"Thank you," I mumble into the phone, then drop it back onto the cradle, an unexpected knot forming in my stomach.

Without so much as a good-bye, my husband has left Las Vegas.

CHAPTER FIVE

The Real World

Aubree

Today is the most Monday of Mondays to ever Monday.

After my long weekend in Vegas, all I want to do is put on a face mask, drink a cup of tea, and detox from all the noise, glitter, and bad decisions. Instead, I'm sitting at my desk with the biggest latte the coffee shop down the street could legally sell me without it being a health hazard, wondering, A) if I should have taken another vacation day to recover from traveling, and, B) if I fell asleep at my desk, would anyone notice?

Unfortunately, the answer to both of those questions is a big fat *yes*.

I've spent my entire professional career working for this charity organization. When I was fresh out of college, they hired me on as an intern to sort mail and work the tables at charity events. But I've spent the eight years since then climbing up the ranks, and now I'm in charge of everything related to fund-raising.

Thanks to my department, our organization serves tons of underprivileged kids in the city, making hockey accessible to families who couldn't otherwise afford extracurricular sports. And while I've spent the last eight years being overworked and underpaid, it's all worth it when I meet the kids who attend our athlete-led camps, and get to watch their eyes light up when they meet their heroes.

Unfortunately, not every day on the job is as magical as that. For example, today.

I'm scrolling through our database of new do-nors, all of whom need to receive a handwritten thank-you note. But my mind is anywhere but here. Mostly, it's on the diamond ring that I slipped off and hid in my dresser drawer, and whether Landon will ever respond to me so we can discuss it. Plus, I want to apologize for freaking out and bolting at the news that he's a virgin. But it's kind of hard to do that when I can't even get a text back.

I eye the thick stack of thank-you notes on my desk, wondering if I should resort to snail mail to get in touch with him. What would I write? *Thank you so much for your donation of this enormous diamond ring. Now, can we freaking talk about this?*

My mini freak-out is delayed by a familiar cheerful voice coming from just outside my office door.

"Welcome back, Aubree."

David Stone, the director of the organization, is standing in my doorway, shooting me a big warm smile. If he weren't my boss and also the single most likable guy on the planet, I'd probably shoo him away in an effort to skip the small talk and get some work done. But he's both of those things, so I push my stack of thank-you cards aside.

"How was Vegas?" he asks, staying put until I wave him inside. The guy is almost too polite.

"It was . . . Vegas. Nothing big to report," I lie. If possible, I'd like to keep the whole drunken-marriage-to-a-player info as far away from the office as I can. News like that has a way of getting out, but the longer I can put it off, the better.

"There's actually something I wanted to talk to you about." David eyes the plush blue chair across from my desk. "Mind if I take a seat?"

I nod, sitting up a little straighter as he settles in across from me. "What's up?"

Instead of an answer, I get another question. "Have you ever been to Vancouver?"

I shake my head. "I've never even left the country. Why do you ask?"

"I've been in talks with a youth hockey organization there," he says. "Great program. Or at least, it was. Their executive director recently passed away, and things have been pretty scattered for them ever since. It's been a year now, and they still haven't been able to get it sorted. Anyway, they reached out to us about absorbing their programs, along with their donors. They do incredibly similar work to us, with one major difference." He pauses for dramatic effect, then adds, "It's entirely for girls."

My eyes widen in interest. "Really? That's incredible."

"I couldn't agree more," David says, a confident grin stretching across his face. "Which is why I think you're the perfect person to lead the expansion."

My breath catches in my throat. "Lead? What do you mean?"

"Be in charge, take the reins, steer the ship!" His smile is huge.

I gnaw on the inside of my cheek, resisting the urge to ask David if he recently bought a thesaurus. "Why me?"

His tone becomes more serious. "I know how passionate you are about underprivileged kids, and sports, and you've been with us for coming up on a decade now. You know this organization backward and forward. This could be your perfect next step."

I fumble for the right words, but my brain is a mess of questions. The only sentence I can formulate is an incomplete one, and it comes out slow and uncertain. "But . . . Vancouver?"

David nods firmly. "You'd have to relocate. But it's only a three-and-a-half-hour drive away. And we'd cover your cost of moving."

My gaze flickers from David to the walls of my office, trying to soak in all the memories I've made here over the past eight years.

"It sounds like the opportunity of a lifetime," I say honestly, "but I'll have to think about it." It's a non-answer, but it's all I can manage right now.

"I need you for this, Aubree," he says, his expressive eyes imploring mine.

David Stone is a difficult man to say *no* to, and he knows it. He's like a golden retriever in khakis. Everyone loves the guy—me included. After all, he taught me everything I know. Plus, he's kind and trustworthy, and a great boss.

"There's no one else I trust," he adds.

"It sounds amazing," I hear myself saying as blood thunders in my ears.

But what about Landon?

But nothing, the sassy part of my brain snaps.

It was a drunken Vegas mistake.

Wasn't it?

It doesn't matter that the night we spent together was fun. It does matter that he's so damn attractive it makes my stomach hurt. Marrying Landon in some quickie ceremony was the stupidest thing I could have done.

So, why does his presence in my life feel like the only thing I have to look forward to right now? I mean, the idea of spending more time in his intoxicatingly masculine presence is much more enticing than, well . . . anything else.

But I don't dare tell my boss. I can't.

I respect David, I really do, but leaving a city I love and all the friendships I've built to move to a foreign country? The idea of it leaves me reeling.

It's only Canada, I tell the part of my brain that's spinning. *It's only a few hours away.*

When I realize David's still talking, I drag my attention back to him.

"Expanding the mission, impacting the lives of female athletes in the making . . . we can't afford not take this shot."

I nod.

"And I need my best employee on this expansion. I won't be there for daily supervision or oversight. You'd be in charge of getting the whole operation off the ground—managing the thing top to bottom."

"It's a tremendous opportunity."

He smiles warmly. "I'm glad you think so. It will also come with a nice promotion too. A change in title and a pay increase commensurate with your new responsibilities. It's always been my dream to push further to do more and impact more lives. And now we have a chance to do that."

"That's great," I hear myself saying.

He nods. "I need someone I can trust at the helm of our first *international* operation." He grins like he's pleased with the sound of that.

"I don't know what to say." I squeeze my knees under my desk where he sits in front of me with a scrutinizing gaze. David has been a widower for nearly two decades. He lives and breathes this job because of it. He's a great boss, and very hard to say no to.

David smiles at me expectantly. "Say yes."

"Um, yes," I say slowly, still in shock.

"Perfect. We'll talk details soon." He stands up and strolls away with a satisfied expression, while my stomach is in knots.

This opportunity is all I've been working toward—better pay, more responsibility, and, of course, the idea of impacting more people as we take the charity international. It's just—wow. Of course I'm excited, but everything feels so unsettled, which is something I've been feeling a lot lately. My life feels like one giant knot I need to untangle.

But for now, it will have to wait. There are

thank-you notes to write.

I pop in my earbuds and get in a full half hour of work before the next interruption. This time, it's a welcome one, a text from my friend Ana.

Do you have any lunch plans?

Nope.

Perfect. Meet me in 30 at that new ramen place?

Damn her—tempting me with spicy noodles.

You just want all the dirty details from Vegas.

I click SEND on my message and barely have to wait ten seconds for her reply.

Girl, you know I do, and you'd better not hold out on me.

Ana has been one of my closest friends and most consistent yoga buddies for the last year. We met right after she moved here from her hometown of Las Vegas to live with her Hawks defenseman boyfriend, Jason Kress. He's kind of an outcast and doesn't hang out much with the team.

But even though Jason and Ana weren't part of the Vegas festivities, I have little doubt that conversation about the rookie's brand-new marriage has dominated the locker-room chatter. Even if it is the off-season, and a lot of the guys are off taking much-needed vacations, plenty of them are still around—hitting the weight room with gusto, working with team personal trainers on plans to improve weaknesses before training camp begins. There's little doubt in my mind that both Landon and Jason are among them. And if Jason knows, then Ana knows. I have a sinking feeling that this lunch offer on Monday is coming from the kindness in her heart.

I'm not sure if I should just go and get this over with or avoid it altogether. But then again, Justin and Elise have jetted off to hike Machu Picchu while Sara and TK are in the Virgin Islands for the next ten days. Which means I do need some girl-friend time, so I should probably take Ana up on her offer for ramen, even if she is going to pump me for information. Plus, some outside advice might not be the worst thing in the world. And, really, my love of spicy noodles can't be underestimated. I love me some carbs.

So I text her back.

Fine. I'll be there. But be nice.

I'm always nice, Ana replies.

Ugh. She really is, so I can't even argue the point.

• • •

"Is it true?" Ana's shiny brown ponytail swings as she tilts her head, waiting for an answer to the question she's asked me three times now.

The restaurant is packed to capacity with the lunchtime crowd, but we were able to snag a tiny table for two in the back, barely large enough to hold our two big plastic bowls of ramen. But while all my focus is on my green curry shrimp and delicious noodles, Ana is much more interested in the train wreck that was my weekend in Vegas.

If there were any doubts as to whether she's caught wind of my marital status shift, they were cleared up the instant we sat down and she pointed out that, while there's no ring on my finger, there is an indent where one used to be. Sometimes I think she'd make a better detective than a massage therapist.

With my expert chopstick-handling skills, I pick up a shrimp and several noodles and pop them into my mouth. It's more than I can comfortably chew, but that will keep me from being able to answer questions, right?

Ana's caramel-colored eyes bore into me, squinty and suspicious. "Just because you have a mouth full of ramen doesn't mean you don't have to spill the deets."

I blink up at her, one noodle hanging out of my mouth, and grumble some nonsense from behind closed lips. She laughs, which was my goal, but it's not enough for her to ditch her one-woman crusade for information. Unfortunately.

"Eventually, you're going to get to the bottom of that." She nods toward my red plastic bowl of noodles. "And then you'll be out of excuses. So you might as well just tell me now."

I gulp down both my noodles and my pride. "Fine. It's true. Landon and I got married."

Ana lets out an excited squeal, which is the opposite of the reaction I was hoping for.

"It's not legit," I hiss, trying to quiet her down.

I don't need the whole restaurant staring. "Well, I mean, it is legit in that it's legally binding. But he was drunk, and I was, well, drunker. It's not like I actively made the decision."

"But your subconscious thought it was a good idea to marry him!" Ana says, a little louder than I'd prefer.

"When I'm drunk, my subconscious also thinks it's a good idea to eat half a pizza at two in the morning," I say stubbornly. "And I think you, me, and the cellulite on my ass all know there's nothing smart about that."

She shrugs. "I don't know about that. I'm pretty much always pro-pizza."

I frown, pointing an accusatory chopstick at her. "If our yoga instructor knew what a bad influence you are, she'd never let you back in class again."

Okay, yeah, she would. Ana's a freaking size two and gorgeous. She's such a brat.

"Don't change the subject. You were about to tell me all about your wedding night."

I lean my chopsticks on the side of my bowl, sighing in defeat. There's no way I'm going to get around telling her. And maybe it'll feel good to get some of it off my chest.

I take a deep breath. "So, like I said, we'd both been drinking."

Ana props her elbows on the table and leans in, eager to hear more. "That's how all good stories start."

I give her the full recap of the evening, or at least what I can remember of it, and the unfortunate morning after where I nearly hyperventilated in front of him.

She swoons at the details of him helping me calm down, despite me trying to downplay anything even remotely cute about this story. I need her on my side, Team Common Sense. She should be rooting for me to get this annulment and go back to the way things were, before I knew details like how good of a kisser Landon is, and how fooling around with him, even with all of our clothes still on, was steamier than pretty much all the sex I've had in my life put together.

"The point is," I say in conclusion, folding my hands on the table, "with our age difference and our insanely different lives, it's ridiculous to think that things could actually work out between us, right?"

Ana twirls a noodle around her chopsticks, mulling it over, then shrugs. "I kinda think it's romantic that he's not willing to let this go."

Exasperated, I sigh. "He's not romantic. He's a child, Ana. He's only twenty-three."

She disagrees with a shake of her head. "Twenty-three is old enough to vote, serve your country, drink, play a professional sport, get hitched in Vegas, and it's most definitely old enough to fall in love."

Grabbing my ice water, I take a long sip, hoping it will extinguish some of the turmoil inside me.

"Make whatever excuses you want," she says, "and if you don't feel anything for him, fine. But don't blame any of this on his age."

I purse my lips. "You might be right. I sound like a jaded old bitch."

She chuckles. "You don't, Aubree. I just think you could at the very least date the poor guy. He is your husband, after all."

"I really wish everyone would stop saying that!" I shout just as our server appears to check on us. I fake smile up at him and pretend to not be crazy, because what's the alternative?

Ana grins at me when he leaves. "Besides, surely there are perks to dating a younger man. I mean, his stamina and recovery time alone must be particularly impressive." She gives me a conspiratorial wink, her grin crooked.

"I, um, wouldn't know," I grumble, feeling even worse.

Her face falls. "Oh. I just assumed you guys had, ya know?" Her eyebrows wiggle. "Hooked up."

I'm sure everyone assumes that, and I haven't corrected them. It's really not my place to out Landon's choice to remain celibate. If he hasn't broadcasted it to our circle of friends, I assume he doesn't want it shared. And it's a secret I'm happy to protect for him, husband or not. It's the decent thing to do.

"We didn't, actually. We were both wasted, stumbling over ourselves," I say. It's true enough, so I don't feel bad lying.

Ana nods. "Makes sense. Maybe you need to, you know, take him for a spin then." She can't even keep a straight face while suggesting it, but when I roll my eyes, her tone turns serious. "I mean it.

There's no harm in seeing if you have a physical connection. What do you have to lose?"

"Nothing," I admit reluctantly. Little does she know that Landon is the one with everything to lose. I'm sure he doesn't want to give it all up for me when this has almost no chance of lasting, and I honestly wouldn't want him to.

After we settle the bill and slurp down what's left of our ramen, Ana and I hug good-bye and head in our separate directions.

But for the rest of the day, her words ring through my head. I know she thinks I should give Landon a shot, but it's not that simple. Yes, he's gorgeous and easy to talk to when he isn't being a total pain in the ass about this whole marriage fiasco, but there are a million reasons why we'd be a bad idea. Especially now that I've said yes to moving out of the country.

It would never work in the long run, and one of us would end up hurt. Maybe me. Or maybe him, when he realizes he gave up everything for me.

CHAPTER SIX

Restless

Landon

I spent all day Monday getting my ass kicked by my trainer, and then endured an excruciating sports massage by the team's masseur, aptly nicknamed Thor. All in all, it was a good day.

There's nothing that centers me more than some good old-fashioned hard work, yet still I can't shake the feeling that something's off. I'll give you one guess about what that *thing* might be. A certain five-foot-nothing feisty brunette named Aubree Derrick. And now the idea of going home alone to an empty apartment, well, let's just say it's the last thing I want to do. A root canal would rank higher, quite frankly.

I haven't seen her since Saturday, when we spent the night together in the honeymoon suite.

She messaged me late Sunday, asking if I'd gotten home okay, but I haven't replied yet. Mostly because I had no clue what to say.

We had a good time that night, but when things got heated between us and I told her I've been waiting for the right girl, she extracted herself from my lap so quickly, I was surprised she didn't pull a muscle. And then she all but sprinted from the hotel room, calling out for me to have a good night. It wasn't exactly my dream scenario.

Checking the time, I'm guessing she'll be off work soon. With a restless sigh, I pull out my phone and type out a text to Aubree.

Hey. I don't know your schedule, but I'm wondering if you have time to meet for a drink or dinner tonight, or maybe coffee tomorrow. I would like to see you.

After a shower, I see she's replied, and as I fumble to unlock my phone screen, my mouth quirks up in a smile.

Hey, I could meet for a quick drink after work if you like?

Absolutely. You work in Bell-

```
                          town, right?
```

```
     Yes  .  .  .
```

I'm guessing she's wondering how I knew that fact. But I've paid closer attention to Aubree than she probably realizes.

```
There's  a  place  I  like  called
Fancy Jacks over there. You want
                         to try it?
```

Her reply comes quickly. `Sounds  good.` `See  you  there  at  6.`

The idea of seeing Aubree tonight has me all kinds of excited. But I'm probably not supposed to admit that.

For half a second, I stand in front of my closet in nothing but black boxer briefs, considering what to wear. But *fuck it*. I'm being ridiculous. Settling on a pair of dark jeans and a worn gray T-shirt, I dress quickly and then slip my feet into a pair of sneakers before heading out.

Aubree's already there when I arrive, seated at the bar, facing away from me. But I'd recognize her heart-shaped ass and the tumble of dark waves down her back from any angle. My breath catches in my throat as I head closer.

She has a glass of red wine and an ice water in front of her. I pause beside the bar until her gaze swings over to mine.

"Hey." She smiles, looking gorgeous dressed in fitted black pants, a pink silk blouse, and nude-colored high heels.

"Hey." I pull out the stool next to hers and take a seat.

"Here's the drink menu. I wasn't sure what you wanted." Aubree hands me a piece of cardstock that has various craft beers and specialty cocktails listed, and her fingers brush mine, sending heat crackling up my arm.

I almost want to say something funny to break the ice, like, *How was your day, honey?* But somehow I doubt Aubree would laugh. Her expression is serious, her eyes guarded.

So I settle on, "How was work?"

"Busy." She exhales. "It looks like I'm going to be taking the lead on a new project, which means some extra hours until it's all sorted out."

"Is that . . . good?"

She shrugs, looking down at her hands. "That's what they tell me."

The bartender appears, and I order a draft beer. I never drink during the season, but off-season is a different story. I can have a beer or two without having to worry about how it will affect my performance in the morning. I know some of the guys aren't as disciplined, but my season wasn't all that stellar, so I can't afford any mishaps.

"You do anything interesting today?" she asks as the bartender sets a frosty glass of beer in front of me.

"I worked out. Skated. Got a massage. Went home and took a shower, then I texted you."

She sighs. "I'm jealous. A massage sounds amazing."

"Eh, don't be jealous. A sports massage and stretching by our team masseur is anything but enjoyable."

She chuckles.

"The happy hour menu, if you guys are interested," the bartender says, placing a couple of menus in front of us.

"Have you eaten?" I ask Aubree as I scan the

menu.

"No, but I'm not hungry."

"I'm ordering food. You need to eat."

"I just said I'm not hungry."

Our eyes meet and fire burns between us. "You also just said you haven't eaten, ergo, I'm feeding you."

She leans in, the fire burning brighter in her eyes. "Look, Landon, I appreciate the fact that you're trying, but you don't actually think this is going to work, do you?"

"Think what's going to work? Are you talking about suggesting you eat because you haven't? Or are we going straight into talking about us?" I ask, dropping my voice and loving the pink tinge that hits her cheeks.

"Us," she whispers. "I'm not sure what you meant before . . . but you don't actually think we're going to work, do you?"

"I don't know, and I won't know unless we try. Would it really be the worst thing in the world to see where it goes?" I want to take away the worry in her eyes, but that's hard to do when she won't let me in.

With a defeated sigh, Aubree picks up her menu. And when the bartender swings back by, we place our order.

"Tell me more about your work," I say, taking a sip of the beer in front of me.

Aubree looks down at her hands, going momentarily quiet. "I love what I do," she says after a few seconds of silence.

When I probe more, she launches into a story about a program she's designed called Little Rookies Camp, which will be for kids ages six to twelve and is geared at reducing childhood obesity and also creating lifelong hockey fans. The program will be completely free to the public and held a few times a quarter. Right now, she's working on securing donors to supply all the equipment—helmets, pads, skates, and sticks—since it will be provided to the kids free of charge.

"That sounds awesome."

We make small talk while we eat, hitting on a wide variety of topics from our childhoods to our favorite books to our favorite foods. She's easy to talk to, and I'm having more fun than I anticipated.

I guess I was worried tonight would be awkward. It's the first time I've seen her since Vegas, but thankfully it's not awkward. Far from it. I find myself leaning closer, looking into her eyes, captivated by her. I also love that she insisted she wasn't hungry, and then took down a whole burger and is now working on my fries.

"*Annie* can't be your favorite movie," I say on a groan.

"It is." She nods, dragging her fry through the ketchup on my plate.

I guess movies are just one more thing we can't agree on. No big surprise there.

"Fine. What's yours?" she asks.

"*Shawshank Redemption*, obviously. I'm not a monster, Aubree."

This pulls a laugh from her. "You're *something* . . ."

The soft feeling inside my chest is entirely unexpected. I like sitting here with her, sharing a meal, bickering over things. It feels domestic. Natural.

It's time to ask the question that's been on the tip of my tongue since I got here. "Why did you rush out of my room that night in Vegas?"

"What do you mean?" she asks, pausing with a

fry in her hand.

I smirk, knowing full well that she knows exactly what I'm talking about. "Well, I for one liked the kissing."

She chuckles, setting down her food and wiping her hands on a napkin. "I liked the kissing too, but . . ." She pauses, her face flushing.

"But what?"

On a deep inhale, Aubree leans a little closer. "I haven't had sex in a very long time, and I . . ." With a nervous chuckle, she waves her hand. "I'm going to stop talking now."

My mouth twitches with a smile. *Damn*, she's cute when she's nervous. If I'm reading between the lines, I take her comment to mean that she liked what we were doing and her body wanted more, but she was trying to be respectful of my boundaries. It's kind of hot, to be honest.

"I wasn't sure where the line was," she says, her voice coming out soft.

And she didn't want to cross it. Again, hot.

"I'm not a saint. Never claimed to be."

"So, we could have done other things," she

murmurs, her brain obviously working.

"I'm a big fan of other things."

"Are you now?" She chuckles.

"I'm actually president of the fan club."

After this, the bartender swings by.

Once I slip a couple of bills into the leather portfolio, I ask her, "You ready to get out of here?"

She nods, gathering her purse. "Thanks for dinner. I probably would have eaten an entire bag of popcorn when I got home, if it weren't for you."

"No worries. That's what I'm here for."

Outside on the sidewalk, I wait with her for the valet to bring her car. When the small silver sedan stops next to the curb, she nods.

"That's me."

I walk her to the car, and the valet hops out, leaving the door open. Aubree looks up at me expectantly.

I'm unsure on the protocol here, and I don't want to push her, but I do want to kiss her. I lean in and give her a hug, and when Aubree wraps one arm around my shoulders, her fingers brushing the hair at the back of my neck, it sends sensation tingling down my spine.

She studies me as if she's unsure what to do or say next. But there's no playbook, no analytical reasoning that could make this situation between us make sense. So I follow my instincts, bringing my lips to hers for a sweet, slow kiss.

"Good night," I murmur.

"Night," she says softly.

Then I watch her drive away, my heart still beating fast from that kiss.

• • •

When I get home, the newest rookie, Jordie, is standing outside my building, looking at his phone.

Fuck. I forgot I'd invited him over to play video games tonight. I guess it goes to show how distracted I've been since returning from Vegas.

"You're late," he says when I approach.

"Sorry, dude. Were you waiting long?"

He shakes his head as I use my keycard to buzz us in through the front doors. "Nah. Five minutes, tops."

Inside the elevator, Jordie launches into a story about the pair of best friends he met last night, who he swears wanted to take turns sharing him. I'm pretty sure he's full of shit. Then again, who the hell knows. I only met Jordie two weeks ago after he got called up from our minor league affiliate. But since we're both younger than most of the guys on the team, I figured I'd reach out to him and invite him over.

Jordie—aka Jordan Prescott, number ninety-one, and the Ice Hawks' newest left winger—folds his lanky frame onto my sofa and grabs the video game controllers while I go to the kitchen for a couple of beers. I'm really not in the mood for company tonight, but maybe kicking his ass in *Madden* would distract me from my situation with Aubree.

"So, is it true?" He looks toward me, smirking. "Did you actually get hitched in Vegas?"

Then again, maybe not.

I select my team and keep my eyes on the TV screen. "Yeah, the rumors are true."

Jordie chuckles. "So, what's the annulment process like? Is it like it is in the movies?"

"I wouldn't know. I haven't even looked into

it yet."

Jordie's expression is stunned. "Uh, okay. But you're going to, right?"

With a sigh, I keep my gaze on the screen. "What are you, my therapist? Do you want to talk all night, or do you want to play?"

He shoots me an easy grin. "Fine, let's play. But prepare to get your ass whupped."

"We'll see about that, rookie."

This I can deal with—trash talk and video games—because I've already decided against saying anything more to Jordie. Number one, I don't know him all that well, so there's no reason to spill my soul. And, two, I really don't know where my head's at, to be honest.

Well, that's not entirely true. I may be young, but I know what I want. I want all the things I never had growing up.

Someone to come home to each night. Loyalty. Comfort. Family dinners. Real holiday traditions, instead of tagging along to a relative's house of whichever woman my dad happened to be dating that Christmas. Or worse, when he wasn't seeing anyone and then we'd stay home alone, eating a frozen dinner on the couch. At least when we were invited to tag along with his girlfriend's family, there would be homemade dessert after dinner. Flag football in the yard.

That's not to say my dad treated me poorly or was a terrible father—he wasn't. I always had lunch money and new hockey skates when I outgrew the pair I'd been skating in. We just didn't have much of a connection, and there was a lot of turmoil in his personal life, which I watched from the sidelines. My mom lived a few hours away, and I only saw her a few weekends a year.

As we play, or to be fair, as I get my ass handed to me in *Madden NFL*, I mentally make a pros-and-cons list about Aubree as wife material. She's smart, hardworking, and funny. She's definitely the type of girl I'd be proud to take home to meet my mom and dad.

The conversation at dinner flowed easily between us, but it wasn't forced. Girls my age talk a lot. One thing I've noticed about Aubree—she only speaks when she has something insightful to say. It's refreshing. When we do chat, I usually learn something, or come away with a deeper understanding. It's nice, definitely a quality I'd like in a partner. Another tick mark goes into the pros column.

When Jordie goes to take a piss, I grab my phone and text Aubree.

> Thank you for tonight.

Her reply comes a second later.

> I should be the one thanking you for dinner.

I smile, recalling how she dug into her burger, moaning at the first bite.

> It was my pleasure.

I can't believe I'd never been there before. It's only two blocks from my office.

> Are you free this Saturday? I text her, then think, Way to cut to the fucking chase, Covington. I practically hold my breath, waiting for her reply.

> I am . . . Why? What did you have in mind?

My heart thumps steadily as I quickly type out

my response.

`I need your help with something.`

`I'm intrigued . . .` is her only reply.

`Saturday at noon,` I tell her. `It's a`
                                  `date.`

`Okay,` she texts back.

With a grin, I pocket my phone just as Jordie comes strolling out of the kitchen, carrying another two bottles of beer.

"Another game?" he asks.

"Sure. Why not?"

With my thoughts still on Aubree, I settle onto the couch for a rematch.

Maybe the solution to all of this is easier than I thought. I married the girl . . . shouldn't I at least date her?

CHAPTER SEVEN

A Normal Married Couple

Aubree

No matter how long and tiring the work week is, my Saturday morning yoga class is a beacon of light at the end of the tunnel. A whole hour dedicated to calming myself with deep breathing and thoughtful meditation. And this week, I need it even more than usual. My instructor would probably say I'm feeling *unbalanced*. I would say I'm feeling totally out of whack.

While my toes are gripping the mat, grounding me in warrior pose, my mind is wandering fast and furious toward my date with Landon this afternoon. I'm so freaking relieved that he reached out to me earlier this week, and that the disappearing act I pulled when he told me he was a virgin didn't make him hate me forever.

I may not be sold on the husband-and-wife thing, but I care about him and would never forgive myself if he thought I'd judged him. I was sure I'd scared him away, but by the way he kissed me when we said good-bye after our date, I think he wants to stick around. And that's even scarier.

"Take a deep breath in, and now exhale all of your distractions and anxieties," the instructor guides us, and I do as I'm told.

I'm 90 percent sure the woman is reading my mind. That or the fact that I'm toppling out of half-moon pose is giving me away.

Focus, Aubree. Only fifteen minutes of class left to go.

Despite my chronically wandering mind, I make it through class and actually manage to feel a little more relaxed at the end. But when I grab my purse out of the cubby and see I have a text from Landon, I'm right back where I started. Especially because this isn't just a *hey, how are you* kind of text. It's a text asking me to wear my ring when I come over today.

My mouth turns dry as I stare down at my phone, then at my naked left hand. I haven't taken the ring out of the jewelry box since I put it there

Monday morning.

At first, I told myself I'd just take it off for work to keep the gossip to a minimum, but every time I thought about putting it back on, it just felt wrong. But he must have noticed that I wasn't wearing it when we met up the other night, and now I feel like the jerk of the century. Not only did I flee when I found out my husband was a virgin, but now I'm not wearing the obscenely expensive ring he bought me. I'm certainly not going to be winning any Wife of the Year awards anytime soon.

As I walk through the parking lot to my car, I formulate an apology text.

```
I'm sorry I haven't been wear-
ing it. I love the ring, I just
                  need time.
```

Once I hit SEND, the three bubbles pop up almost instantly as he texts me back.

```
I know, that's fine. But I have
someone from my insurance compa-
ny coming by to do an appraisal
so we can get a policy on it, so
I need you to bring it.
```

`Oh, of course!` I reply, feeling relieved,

but also a little foolish. Of course he wants to insure it. It's worth a lot of money.

After a shower, I blow-dry my hair, swipe on a few coats of mascara, and tug on jeans and an emerald-green top that's as comfy as it is cute. Then I'm back in my car, cruising toward Landon's apartment downtown. He buzzes me up, and while I'm still in the elevator, my phone dings with a text from him.

Door is unlocked. Walk right on in, wifey.

I roll my eyes at the *wifey* part but follow instructions, turning the doorknob of his top-floor apartment extra slowly, just in case I got the apartment number wrong. When I spot a duffel by the door with the Ice Hawks logo and a big number 94 printed on the side, I swing the door all the way open and step inside.

"Knock, knock," I call out as I step through the large open foyer and admire his state-of-the-art kitchen. It's a nice apartment, although he clearly hasn't lived here long. The only non-necessity in the living room is the enormous flat-screen TV mounted on the wall. Although, based on the tangle of cords from various video-game consoles, Landon might consider that more of a necessity than a luxury.

"Be there in a sec," his deep voice calls from somewhere inside the apartment.

I turn to find Landon coming down the hallway, dressed in a pair of dark well-fitting jeans and a black T-shirt that stretches distractingly across his muscular chest. My stomach does a little flip when his eyes meet mine. They're a brilliant shade of blue, like the Puget Sound at sundown.

"Thanks for coming." His lips twitch at the sight of me in his apartment.

There's no denying it. He's cute. Polite. Kind eyes. Midwestern good-boy vibes. Charming, even when he doesn't mean to be. It could mess with a girl.

Good thing I'm not a girl anymore. Haven't been for a long time. But when will I start feeling like a full-fledged adult, capable of making adult decisions, like—oh, I don't know—insisting on an annulment of this crazy union? Because so far, I don't seem capable.

And I'm here, on a date, with my totally hunky husband.

"Something to drink?" he asks, breaking the drawn-out silence between us.

"Sure." I shrug and watch Landon's retreating form as he heads for the kitchen.

"This is so nice," I say, referring to both the apartment and the view of his perfectly firm hockey player butt.

Crossing the room, I take a seat on the tan couch, one of the few pieces of furniture in the space. Moments later, Landon joins me, handing me a can of ginger ale.

"Do you just keep these around?" I ask, accepting the chilled drink from him and tugging at the pop tab until it snaps open.

"No, I picked up some just in case last night. You were drinking it in the honeymoon suite, so I figured you liked it."

I suppress a smirk. "I was drinking ginger ale in Vegas because I was hung over, not because it's my all-time favorite drink." When I notice the disappointment in his eyes, I quickly add, "But I was actually in the mood for ginger ale today, so thank you," which cheers him up enough to put the light back in his bright blue eyes.

It really was sweet for him to remember my beverage choice. No one has cared enough to notice the tiniest details about me in a long time.

A knock at the door brings Landon to his feet again. "That must be the appraiser."

He grabs a stack of papers off the coffee table, then heads for the door, welcoming in a slim woman with jet-black hair that matches her black pantsuit and pumps. She's striking, and the way she smiles at Landon makes me feel surprisingly defensive. Springing to my feet, I shake her hand and introduce myself.

An enormous smile spreads across her face, as though ring insurance were the most exciting thing in the world. "You two are a gorgeous couple. I'll bet your wedding pictures are like something straight out of a bridal magazine."

I smile while biting my tongue. If only she knew the only pictures we have are blurry ones that our drunk friends took on their cell phones. "Let's get this appraisal done, shall we?"

The three of us settle in the living room, and Landon hands over the stack of paperwork he's been clutching.

"Here's the receipt, and the copy of the certificate of authenticity you requested."

The appraiser nods, running one red nail along the details printed on the page. Three carats. Platinum setting. All the things a girl dreams her ring will be. Unbuckling her briefcase, she slips the papers away and hands Landon a pen, along with a few documents to sign.

"While you review those, I'll just need to take a quick look at the ring itself."

Reluctantly, I shimmy the ring off my finger and place it in her palm. Despite the fact that I haven't worn it all week, I feel naked the second I take it off. Like a crucial part of me is missing. My eyes stay glued on her as she inspects the center diamond, jotting down notes on the color and cut.

"So, when was the big day?" she asks, her gaze still firmly locked on my ring. Thank God she doesn't look up at me, or she would see that I have to squint and rack my brain to come up with the date.

"A week ago from yesterday? So that would've been . . . June twelfth, right?" I look to Landon for confirmation, but he has his nose buried in paperwork, seemingly as uncomfortable with this question as I am.

"A June wedding. Great choice."

I'm sure she's envisioning peonies and a sunny outdoor ceremony, and I'm not about to correct her. "Yep, we love the summertime."

The words feel foreign in my mouth. *We* love the summertime. As if Landon and I have known each other long enough to share an opinion on favorite seasons.

"Such a perfect time of year for a honeymoon too," she says, returning the ring to me. "Where did you two go?"

"We, um, we actually didn't have one," I say, sliding the ring back on. Suddenly, I find myself very interested in picking at my nail polish. Anything to avoid eye contact with this nosy Nancy.

"Delayed honeymoon," she says, nodding as if it all makes sense. "I've heard they're super trendy right now. Gives you something to look forward to, right?"

"That's right," Landon says, sliding the stack of signed papers across the coffee table. "Is there anything else you need?"

The appraiser flips through the paperwork, verifying Landon has signed every dotted line before tucking it into her briefcase. "That should be it. Short and sweet. I hope I didn't delay your weekend plans."

Landon shakes his head as he pushes to his feet, cueing us to do the same. "We're just going shopping today. I need to get this place furnished." He tilts his head toward the sparsely decorated space. "If you hadn't noticed."

She laughs politely, then cranes her neck to take in the bare apartment. "There's a lot you can do with this space. I can just see it with an old oak hutch full of your wedding pictures, maybe even a high chair at the kitchen table." She gives me a wink that makes my stomach lurch.

"We're going to focus on the basics first," I snap, cocking my head and giving her the fakest smile I can muster. She came here to appraise my ring, not to give us family-planning advice.

My sass must be detectable, because she doesn't even bother trying to shake my hand before scurrying out the door. When it clicks closed behind her, the air in the room feels lighter somehow.

"I take it you didn't like her very much." Landon turns toward me with an apologetic look in his eyes, but when he sees my tight-lipped scowl, he laughs. "It's no big deal, Bree. Those are normal questions to ask a married couple."

"A normal married couple," I say, correcting him. "Which we're not."

"As far as anyone else knows, we're a regular all-American bride and groom." He pulls his leather jacket off the back of a chair and tugs it over his muscular arms. "I wasn't kidding about furniture shopping today, though. Are you down?"

I reach for my purse, nodding. Furniture shopping sounds fun. And I doubt the candles and picture frames will ask us about when we're having children.

• • •

Walking into the luxury home store, I feel like somebody should be playing the music from *Annie*. I feel like I'm the little redhead, wandering into Daddy Warbucks' mansion. And I'll admit it. I think I'm gonna like it here.

As I wander the store, running my fingers along the expensive linens and silks, it feels like I'm living out a daydream. I've never spent more than fifty bucks on anything in my apartment. I don't have the budget for it.

But years of honing my thrifting skills have been preparing me for this. My eye for design and ability to find diamonds in the rough is something I'm proud of. And trust me, there's a lot of rough in this store. Just because it's all expensive doesn't mean it's all good. And it takes less than five minutes for it to become glaringly obvious that Landon wouldn't know a quality throw pillow if it hit him in his cute hockey-player butt.

"What about these?" He holds up a set of throw pillows the exact shade of a rotting pumpkin.

I can't help but crinkle my nose in disgust. "You'd better set those down before the ugly starts rubbing off on you."

He sighs, returning them to the shelf, then reaches for a black-and-purple striped pillow.

"Don't even think about it," I warn him, and he yanks his hand back faster than if he'd touched a hot stove.

"What's wrong with those?" His tone is so defensive that for a second, I think we must be looking at different pillows. But, no, sure enough, he's gesturing to the striped nightmares.

"Where did you get your taste from? The clearance rack at a Halloween costume store?"

"Jeez, you don't have to be so mean about it," he grumbles under his breath, shoving his hands into the pockets of his jeans. "I've always lived in pre-furnished apartments before. I'm new to this."

I bite down on my lower lip to hold back any more sassy comments. Maybe I was a little harsh. He is a guy, after all. And a twenty-three-year-old at that. He invited me here to help him, not to hurt his feelings.

"I'm sorry, I was rude. Let's start over. What do you want the vibe of your apartment to be?"

His expression relaxes as he runs a hand over his stubble, mulling over my question. "I just want it to feel like home. Cozy, I guess? I like colors, but apparently the wrong ones, according to you."

I nod along with his suggestions. "We can do color. How about I pick some things out that I think will work, and you can be in charge of, um . . . candles."

He raises one thick brow, a suspicious gleam in his brilliant blue eyes. "So you choose everything, and I take the job I'm least likely to screw up?"

"Pretty much," I say with a shrug. There's no sense in sugarcoating it. "Call it my wifely duties kicking in."

The scrunched look on his face is clearly skeptical, but slowly, he surrenders the cart to me. "Fine. But no way are you just banishing me to candle land while you take full control. I'm coming with you."

Landon follows close behind me as I do a lap around the store, holding up options of different colored curtains, blankets, and placemats. He doesn't argue with me when I suggest a neutral color palette with pops of color, but I do have to talk him down from this weird medieval-looking kitchen table he's convinced he needs.

I'm surprised by how much fun we have doing something as simple as picking out placemats. By the time we're done, our cart is overflowing, and his list of furniture to order for delivery is impressively long.

"You did very well," I tell him as he swipes his credit card, making a purchase that, aside from my ring, is probably the most money he's spent at one time, but he takes it in stride. I guess when your paycheck is seven figures, you don't sweat something as simple as furnishing your home.

"*We* did very well," he says, correcting me. "We're not such a bad team after all."

"As long as you let me take the lead," I tell him, taking as many shopping bags as I can hold in my hands. He snickers, scooping up the rest.

It's a short walk back to his car, and Landon loads his bags inside, then takes each one from me to place it carefully in the trunk.

"Should we set all this stuff up when we get back to your place?" I ask as we drive. I might be a little bit giddy to play interior designer with all his new decor.

"It doesn't just have to be my place, you know." His lips lift into a soft smile as his kind eyes meet mine. "There's plenty of room for two. And it's a lot closer to your office."

My eyes feel like they're about to pop out of my head. "You can't seriously be suggesting that I move in with you."

"What if I am?"

There's not the slightest hint of sarcasm in his tone, and if he looks at me even a second longer with those deep blue eyes, he's going to knock me right over, and I'll start agreeing to things I have absolutely no right to agree with.

I don't know what to say without hurting his

feelings, so I just blurt out the first thing that comes to mind. "Landon, you're being weird."

He gives me a pointed look. "What's weird is a married couple not living together."

"But we're not a normal married couple." I feel like a broken record, but apparently, the concept hasn't gotten through his head.

His nostrils flare as he reins in his frustration with a long, strained exhale. "Fine. We'll discuss it later."

He pulls into the parking garage for his building, but rather than open the trunk when we climb out like I expect, he reaches into his pocket and pulls out a key fob. He clicks it twice, triggering a beep, and the lights flash once on a shiny black SUV parked nearby. I have no choice but to follow him toward the SUV.

"How many cars do you own?" I ask, trying to keep up.

"It's not mine. It's yours."

"Wait, hold up a second. What did you say?"

Landon rolls back his shoulders, looking proud. "It's yours. A gift. All the guys' wives drive nice cars. Call it an official initiation into the Ice Hawks wives club."

I can feel the anger slowly creeping up my throat. "You bought me a car without asking?"

"Um, yeah. That's how gifts work, right?" Frowning, he says, "I thought you'd be more excited about this."

I fold my arms tightly over my chest, fully aware he's unhappy about my reaction. "How can I be excited? I like my car. It has a great safety rating, gets good gas mileage, and I just got good at parallel parking with it. If you would've asked me first, you would've known that."

"Shit, I'm sorry." He grips the back of his neck as he stares down at the gray concrete beneath our feet. "I didn't think about that."

I sigh, uncrossing my arms. I can't bear the sight of him looking so bummed. But this is something we need to talk about.

I walk past him and open one of the back doors, peering inside. "It's a beautiful car, Landon. I just don't understand why you bought it. Was it really just so I would fit in with the WAGs?"

"You want the real reason?"

"Of course. I'll always want honesty from

you."

He sighs, worrying one hand through his messy hair before shifting his gaze toward mine. "I thought you'd look hot driving it."

I scoff. That has to be a joke, right? But once again, there's nothing but sincerity in his brilliant blue eyes. My lips part as I fumble for the right words, but I'm momentarily speechless.

"You okay?" He laughs, raising one thick brow.

"You spent eighty thousand dollars on an SUV because you thought I'd look cute sitting in the driver's seat?"

He nods, as if this whole thing were totally ordinary.

"You're an idiot, you know that?"

"Fuck, come here." He scrubs a hand down his face before turning my body toward his. "I don't know what I'm doing."

"That's obvious." I smirk, somehow feeling pleased by his discomfort. This entire time he's been so in control, so chill about this marriage, while I've been reeling in confusion and not having a clue what the hell I'm doing or how to act.

At the first sign of a smile on my lips, he slides an arm around my waist and tugs me even closer to him. "I'm your idiot." He presses a gentle kiss to my cheekbone, sending a flutter to my chest. "Try with me."

"I am trying," I say defensively.

The faint smile twitching on his lips gives everything away. He knows I'm lying. *Dammit*. Why does he have to be so perceptive?

"We'll get there," he says encouragingly.

I fold my arms over my chest as a foreign feeling twists inside me. I both hate and love his confidence in us.

"Patience is a virtue, Landon," I say softly, feeling shaken.

He smiles again, genuinely this time, and tucks a loose strand of hair behind my ear. "You look cute as hell when you're mad."

And before I have time to pick a fight, his mouth descends on mine.

It's just a kiss, a sweet, slow kiss, but it makes me nervous. His kiss holds the power to unleash a torrent of emotions I don't want to feel, but I'm powerless to say no. I want his firm mouth moving on mine.

I draw in a huge, stuttering breath, forcing my lungs into action. And when my lips part, he teases his tongue inside.

Everything in my lower half clenches. *Dear God . . . this man.* He sucks expertly on my bottom lip, nipping at it gently.

The kiss is over way too soon. Before long, Landon pulls back to meet my eyes with a smirk. I don't have any idea how he manages to rile me up one second and then turn me on the next. It's a heady, potent combination that I may never get sick of.

"Should we go upstairs?" he asks, his voice raspy.

"What about the bags?"

"I can ask my building's concierge to bring them up in a bit."

"Then it looks like we're going upstairs." I smile while my heart pounds out an uneven rhythm.

CHAPTER EIGHT

Sorry, Not Sorry

Landon

I take Aubree's hand, tugging her behind me toward the elevator in my apartment building. She jams her finger against the button several times.

"You know that won't make the elevator come any faster, right?" I chuckle, squeezing her hand.

"Shush your mouth," she says with a crooked smile, meeting my eyes.

Loving how feisty she is, I grin at her. "Thank you for today. For coming with me, I mean."

She nods. "I'm terrified to think what you would have chosen if I wasn't there."

Feeling smug, I shake my head. I'm trying not to feel let down at how quickly she refused my gift—that gift being a luxury SUV, mind you. I only wanted to make her happy, but it seems I have a lot to learn about pleasing my wife.

"Can you stay?" I ask when the elevator door opens on my floor.

With a smile tugging at her lips, Aubree nods. "I suppose I can stay for a little while."

I unlock my apartment and let her inside, pausing by the kitchen. "Something to drink?"

"I'm good," she says, but her body language tells a different story. Her posture is straight, stiff, and she hasn't wandered more than a half-dozen steps inside my apartment.

"Care to tell me what's on your mind?" I ask.

She turns to face me with worry clouding her features. "This is crazy, Landon. That SUV is crazy. All of this is crazy."

"My dad was married four times," I blurt, just tossing it out there. *Nice.*

"What?" Aubree narrows her eyes.

"He jumped from relationship to relationship, swearing it was love, promising it was going to last. But it never did."

"Okay . . ." She shifts, still watching me.

"And he wasn't just some delusional sap. I really think he was convinced each time that this was it. He'd found his soul mate. His person. That he'd finally found *the one.*"

"I take it he's not married now?"

I shake my head. Last time I talked to him, he'd signed up for one of those "silver singles" dating sites.

"Landon, I . . ."

I hold up one hand. "Let me finish."

Her mouth closes, and she gestures for me to go ahead.

Actually, I don't know what else there is to say, because Aubree's right—this is crazy. But love is crazy. And marriage is crazier. Pinning all your hopes and dreams on another person is iffy, at best. People are unreliable. Selfish. There's no way to know if any of it will work.

I lick my lips and meet her eyes. "Nothing's guaranteed. All we have is right now. And I'm trying to figure out this thing between us as we go."

"And you don't want to end up like your father," she says, her voice a little unsteady.

I nod. "Exactly. Because when I find love, I want it to be a forever kind of love. To me, marriage isn't a joke, and that's why I want to give it a real go before we even talk about divorce. I know we started in the most unconventional way and it's cliché as fuck, but I don't want you to assume it's a mistake. Because . . . what if it isn't a mistake?"

Aubree doesn't respond, she just starts toward the living room, walking past me and lightly trailing her fingertips along my forearm as she passes.

I don't know what kind of game she's playing, but she's throwing off signals that make me eager to find out. I'm starting to learn that women are confusing as shit—but in all the best, most delightful ways.

Aubree's standing by the couch, and when I place my hands on her hips and tug her close, her small frame practically melts into my much larger one. For a second, I think she's going to stop me. But she did kiss me in the parking garage, so who the hell knows where her head's at right now?

Pressing her hands against my chest, she gives me a little shove until I fall back onto the couch. She joins me, taking a seat beside me.

"Are you okay?" she asks somberly.

No one's ever asked me that question. Not even my parents. Definitely not my teammates.

Of course I'm okay. Or, at least, I'm expected to be. I'm tough and strong, and I don't need coddling. But something split open in my chest at her words. At the way Aubree's looking at me. At the concern in her voice.

I'm used to being the one who holds things together and picks up the pieces when shit goes south. I've done it so many times when my father needed me. I grew up fast, and apparently have what people like to call an old soul. Even at sixteen, I was the one looking out for my father—mowing the lawn, cooking dinner, reminding him to get up and go to work when another of his relationships inevitably went south. And romantic relationships always did. That was what I learned.

But this one hasn't. At least, not yet.

Is it so bad that I want to enjoy it a little before it does?

"I'm good," I tell her. "Come here. I like you close. You're warm and you smell nice."

She chuckles, moving closer, letting me pull

her into my arms. "You smell nice too." Her lips twitching, she climbs into my lap, straddling my thighs. "Is this okay?"

Oh, hell yeah. "Fine by me."

With my fingers under her chin, I lift her mouth to mine. She hesitates for just a second before kissing me back. She tastes sweet, and when her lips part and I sweep my tongue inside, Aubree makes a little sound of pleasure.

Her hands slip into the hair at the back of my neck and she tugs me closer, eager to chase away any remaining distance between us.

I'm not sure if she expects me to be more aggressive or move faster because of how I am on the ice, but there's no way I'm doing anything other than taking my time with her. I have her here—on my couch, not in my bed—a detail my six-foot-three-inch frame doesn't fail to notice, but still. She's here, and she's so warm and responsive in my arms, greedily sucking on my tongue and moving her hips against mine.

Jesus. That feels good.

The entire lower half of my body operates on instinct, slowly grinding against hers. When I roll my hips, my straining erection presses between her legs in a way that makes Aubree shudder and restlessly whimper in my arms.

"So sexy," I say on a groan when she rocks her pelvis, seeking more friction against me.

Aubree exhales a frustrated sound.

I break the kiss, my lips traveling along the softness of her neck. "Is this okay?" I ask between nibbles of smooth skin.

"So much, yes," she says breathlessly, moving against me.

My hand ventures south, trailing over the soft skin of her stomach until I reach the button on her jeans. "And this?" I pause, my fingers hovering over the button.

"Yeah. Yes." She raises onto her knees to help me out.

It's all the go-ahead I need.

I had no expectations about this happening today. I really just invited her along so I could get to know her better, and maybe to get a female opinion on home furnishings. So this is exceeding all my expectations about our first date.

While I focus on getting Aubree's pants undone, her hands are everywhere—in my hair, gripping my shoulders, touching the stubble on my jaw, ghosting over my abs. It's freaking incredible.

I shove her pants down, but our position prevents me from getting them over her hips.

"One sec." I stand and lift her with me, setting her on her feet only long enough to strip her jeans off.

When she sinks back down onto the couch, I fall to my knees in front of her. She watches me, looking a little unsteady, but her eyes burn with need.

I nudge her knees apart, gliding my hand along the smooth skin of her inner thigh. "You sure this is okay?"

I want my mouth all over her. But even if I've thought about eating her pussy for weeks now, I need her to want it too.

Aubree bites her lower lip and nods, watching me with a hooded gaze.

I peel her panties down her legs and groan. She's perfect. I run my thumb along her smooth pussy, and my dick throbs with agreement. With one hand under her knee and the other gripping her inner thigh, I kiss a path from her hip to the spot between her thighs.

Oh shit, she tastes good.

A rumbled groan escapes my throat. "Fuck . . . you're . . ." I kiss her again, open-mouthed and hungry, and Aubree moans, her hips jolting.

"Oh . . . *wow.*" Her voice is raspy, and her fingers clutch my shoulder, her fingernails biting into my skin.

I almost chuckle at her response. One key benefit to still being a virgin? I eat pussy like a fucking Jedi knight.

Sorry, not sorry.

I add one finger, then two, keeping up with the soft strokes of my tongue. Soon, she loses control, grinding her hips against my face and groaning loudly. I love it.

"You taste so good," I murmur before I give her clit a firm suck.

Aubree's thighs tremble and she clutches my hair, tugging as she starts to come. I can feel her body gripping my fingers, and my cock pulses against my thigh. Sensation riots through me. I don't let up until she's trying to squirm away from me.

"Shit, Landon," she murmurs, coming down from her high as I gather her in my arms, tug her close to my chest, and kiss her temple. "That was incredible."

I touch her hair, her cheek. "You're pretty incredible."

I'm not sure if she's self-conscious about what just happened, but Aubree rises to her feet, her face flushed. Pushing my unsettled feelings aside, I help her into her jeans. Once she's dressed, she lets out a stifled yawn.

I chuckle and tuck her hair behind her ear. "You look sleepy."

She nods. "Maybe just a little."

I remember at our dinner the other night, she told me she's been working extra hours because of a big project she's spearheading for her boss. "Then let's get you home."

"What about that?" She looks down to where my dick is threatening to bust through two layers of fabric to come out to greet her.

"Maybe next time," I say with a rasp. *If I earn it.*

Part of me still can't believe I deserve a girl like her. And yeah, I want her—so badly—but I'm also okay with taking my time. That's not to say I won't be jerking it as soon as she's gone.

She nods. And with another sweet kiss, she knocks down another of my walls.

After Aubree leaves, I fall back onto my bed with a sigh. As hot and eager as I was moments before, now that my apartment is quiet and the heat of the moment has passed, something else has taken up residence in my brain. When I close my eyes, all I can picture is the uncertainty in hers when that appraiser questioned us. Pressing my fingers into my temples, I try to stave off the impending headache I can feel forming.

I had fun with her today, more than I expected to, but that's not to say everything went smoothly.

Buying her a new car? Stupid. I see that now.

Can I afford it? Yes. But that doesn't mean it was wise to put a dent in my bank account—and for what? Showing her I was serious about her in a way that words can't?

The worst part is, I'm not sure she even got that, because I muttered something idiotic about her looking hot in the ride. Which is true, as is the thing I said about the WAGs. All the other players' wives drive a nice car, and it's my responsibility to make sure Aubree does too. Call it my grand gesture, or whatever. Simple, right? Except apparently not, because the car sits untouched, gathering dust in the parking garage beneath my building. Good times.

And yet, maybe I've learned something in all of this, because what Aubree said has stuck with me. I need to learn to communicate better with my wife if I have any hope of making this marriage work.

CHAPTER NINE

Making Mountains out of Molehills

Aubree

Of all the ways to spend my evening after working all day, working on a wedding reception seating chart wouldn't be my first choice.

But as a bridesmaid, when Becca texted me last night pleading for my event-planning expertise, I couldn't say no. And as a human being with taste buds, when she lured me with the promise of splitting a veggie pizza while we work, I told her I'd be there. After spending longer than expected at my dermatologist appointment this morning, I sped over to Becca's place, knowing that veggie pizza was just what the doctor ordered.

Not literally. Although I wish.

Now, as I'm standing in her kitchen staring at the nightmare on her table, I understand why the pizza was a necessary incentive. If I didn't know better, I'd think this was the work of some conspiracy theorist trying to piece together clues from a crime.

"So the coasters represent tables, and each poker chip is a guest," Becca explains, gesturing to the chaos happening on her kitchen table. There have to be almost three hundred poker chips, each one with a name written on it in permanent marker. Apparently, the four-hour flight to Becca's hometown of Dallas isn't enough to stop people from RSVPing *yes* to the wedding of the decade.

I pick up a red poker chip, reading the unfamiliar name scrawled on it. "So this is where all the missing chips from poker night have gone."

A guilty smile tugs at her lips. "Petty theft in the name of wedding planning. Don't tell Asher."

We load up our plates with veggie pizza before settling in at the table, rearranging poker chips and taking hefty bites to fuel us. Since there's spinach on the pizza, that makes it brain food, right?

"If you put Coach Dodd and his wife with the players, you can have all the assistant coaches at the same table," I say, dragging the coach's poker chip from one coaster to another.

"That's what I thought too, but then where do my boss and his wife go?"

Becca is the assistant to the owner of the Ice Hawks, so between her coworkers and Owen's teammates, there are about a hundred hockey-related guests attending this wedding. And that's only a third of the total guest count. I guess everything really is bigger in Texas.

I scrunch my brows and take a big bite of pizza, hoping by the time I finish chewing that I'll have a solution. Sadly, no luck.

Becca sighs, resting her chin in her cupped hands. "Aren't you glad you didn't have to do any of this?"

I shrug, scooting the poker chip with my name on it next to Landon's. "Honestly, it's the sort of thing I always pictured doing. I've gotten plenty of practice with all the galas I've orchestrated for work. I always thought I'd get to put it to use someday for my own wedding."

"You and Landon could always renew your vows," she says. "I mean, if you're staying together, that is. I haven't wanted to bring it up, but I'm dying to know."

I groan, only half mocking her. "Not you too."

"Have you guys been . . . spending time together?" she asks, grinning.

I nod. "A little."

Her smile grows wider. "Like, what? A date?"

My lips twitch with the beginning of a smile.

"Spill it!" She squeals, pushing the poker chips away with the first real excitement I've seen all night.

I can't *not* tell her. So I do.

I launch into the full story—the dinner Landon and I shared, the awkward questions from the ring appraiser, shopping together, the freaking car he bought me . . . and even what happened afterward on his couch. My cheeks heat up at the memory of Landon on his knees in front of me.

I force a deep breath into my lungs, remembering that Becca is still watching me. "But I don't know. It feels like he's trying to force it. Trying to make this marriage stick, when I really don't know what I want." I shake my head. "I hardly know him."

Becca's eyes widen. "Oh yeah, going down on you and buying you an SUV. He sounds like a real monster."

I chuckle despite the deep uncertainty swimming inside me. "Honestly, I have no idea what we're doing. But he's not really willing to just let this go." I fidget nervously, picking at my pizza crust. I should have known I wouldn't get through a day of talking wedding stuff without discussing my own marriage. "But, honestly, I'm a little scared."

"Of what?"

"Of failing," I say on a sigh, staring at my left hand. "If we'd just gotten an annulment right away, we could've put it behind us. But now it's different. If we're going to give it our all and it doesn't work out . . . it'll just hurt that much more. Won't it?"

When I meet Becca's gaze, there's a warm look of understanding in her eyes.

"Being in a relationship is scary," she says. "And there's always a risk in any relationship that things won't turn out how you want. But you're not going to protect yourself by not trying. If you don't try, you might miss out on the best thing to ever happen to you."

My chest tightens as I heave another deep sigh. *God*, I hate it when she's right.

Landon is a sweet guy. He'd do anything for anyone, and just wants people to be happy. Okay, and let's not forget that he's handsome as hell too. Yes, his communication skills could use a little work, but he clearly knows how to treat a woman right. And the sexual connection between us is definitely there. Saturday night reassured me of that much.

Which means . . . maybe I shouldn't be holding back or letting my fears determine what could turn out to be a spectacular future?

"So, what else is new?" she asks after a long, comfortable silence.

Shrugging, I take a sip of the drink in front of me. "Nothing much."

I don't dare tell her about the promotion that I've been offered. I try not to even think about it, or I'll be buried in guilt. Is it even worth trying with Landon when I'll be moving soon? It's a question I don't have the answer to.

It's much easier to listen to Becca talk about wedding planning, peppered with snarky comments about her future mother-in-law. I giggle at all the right times.

One hour and a full veggie pizza later, we have a completed seating chart, and I'm a level of tired I haven't been since the Ice Hawks charity gala last month. It's been a long day, and I have to be up extra early for a meeting about the Vancouver project first thing tomorrow morning.

With a quick hug good-bye, I leave Becca's and head home, forgoing the meal prep I had planned in favor of plopping down on the couch. I haven't even picked out what mindless TV show I want to watch when my phone buzzes with a text from Landon.

What are you doing?

It's nice to know he's thinking about me, but today was so busy, I'm not sure if I'm up for pulling myself together to see him.

I decide to keep it vague. Just laying low.

His response comes almost instantly. Not in the mood for company tonight then?

It's not that. I just had a long day, I reply.

He sends back a string of question marks, looking for more details.

I touch the small bandage on my shoulder beneath my shirt. Maybe I should just tell him. It's not that big of a deal, but knowing Landon, it's the kind of thing he would get upset about if I kept it from him. And he was so open with me about his dad, it would feel weird hiding it. So I take a deep breath and type out my reply.

```
Well, after work I helped Becca
with the wedding seating chart,
and I had a suspicious mole on my
shoulder shaved off this morn-
ing, so I think I'm too tired to
                     hang out.
```

Three seconds later, my phone is ringing. It's him. *That didn't take long.*

"Hi." I chuckle nervously, chewing on my thumbnail.

"What do you mean, shaved off? Are you okay?" His voice is stern.

"Um . . . a biopsy, I guess. To check for melanoma." There's a long silence on the other end of the line. "Um, hello? Landon? Are you there?"

"That's skin cancer," he finally says, his voice strained.

"It's probably nothing," I mumble self-consciously, touching the bandage on my shoulder. "I swear, it's not a big deal."

"Are you okay?"

I realize he already asked me that, but I guess I forgot to answer. "I'm fine. I didn't feel a thing. It's a tiny bit sore now that I'm not numbed up anymore, but as long as I don't move my arm around a lot, it's nothing."

"Why didn't you tell me?" His voice is firm, but laced with concern too.

"I'm telling you now, aren't I?"

He sucks in a quick breath, a telltale sign that he's frustrated with me. "I could have driven you to the appointment and stayed with you during the procedure. You said that I should communicate better with you, but you—"

"It was a routine appointment," I say, cutting him off. "I go every year, and this is the first time there's ever been an issue. I have a lot of freckles, in case you didn't notice. It's good to get them checked on."

"Your freckles are cute," he mumbles distractedly.

"Regardless, I'm okay, and now you know."

He draws in another breath, but this time, he sounds relieved. "I'm glad you told me. I'm sorry for panicking."

"Well, you don't have to worry about me tonight." I wiggle my toes under the blanket, watching the fuzzy pink material shift. "I'll be firmly planted on my couch with a lot of snacks and bad TV."

I can practically hear his smirk through the phone. "Not *Annie*, I hope."

That makes me smile. "Not *Annie*. I save that for special occasions."

"What's more special than having a mole shaved off? I'll be right over."

"You don't have—" I say, but Landon's already ended the call. *Damn it!*

I don't want him making such a big deal of this. I'm older than him, thirty now, which means I have weird moles, and boobs that are two inches lower than I'd prefer, and my stomach is soft and squishy, and my thighs are . . . well, let's not get started on my thighs. The point is, there are weird things happening with my body all the time. If he makes a big commotion about every one of them, he'll be having a full-blown freak-out once a week.

I manage to pull myself off the couch and trudge to my bedroom, where I dab a little concealer under my eyes and spray my roots with dry shampoo. I don't need to look like a supermodel—I couldn't even if I tried—but if I don't want Landon being overdramatic about my situation, I should probably look like I have it a little bit together. Downstairs, I rearrange the pillows on my couch, eyeing the dishes I've yet to put away. It's too late to worry about them now. My doorbell is already chiming.

When I tug open the door, I can hardly see the man I was expecting behind the enormous bouquet of pink roses he's holding in front of his chest.

"Hi there, gorgeous."

"You . . . you bought me flowers?"

Landon peers down at me, smiling. "Of course I did. Now, can I come in, or should I just leave the flowers and the cupcake and go?"

My ears perk up at the mention of a cupcake, but I tap my chin and jut out my lower lip, pretending to think it over. "I guess I can let you in under one condition."

"And that is?"

"You watch *Annie* with me."

He lowers the bouquet, giving me a full look at his gorgeous smile, one adorable dimple proudly on display. "Deal."

Inside, Landon slips out of his black sneakers without untying them, then follows me to the kitchen, where I point him toward the vase on the top shelf.

I can't reach it on my own. Short-girl problems.

While I hold the bouquet, I shamelessly stand back and watch his arms flex as he reaches, his shoulders testing the stretch of his T-shirt's sleeves. I'm actually sort of sad when he grabs the vase and the show is over.

Note to self: Put more things on the highest shelf and ask him to reach for them.

While I snip the stems and arrange the flowers, Landon digs into the brown grocery bag, pulling out a small white box with a chocolate cupcake inside.

"Oh, thank God it's chocolate." I sigh, my mouth already watering.

"Not just chocolate." His smile stretches from ear to ear. "It's a chocolate lava cupcake. I figured that's kind of our thing now."

My jaw drops open at least an inch. "They make those?"

He nods, pride flashing in his bright blue eyes as he unboxes the chocolate treat. I get out a plate and two forks, letting him do the honors of splitting it and enjoying the satisfaction of watching the chocolate spill out. He let me do it last time, after all.

"You really didn't have to do any of this." I gesture to the cupcake, the flowers, and of course, to him. He dropped everything and raced over here without me even asking, all because he wanted to make sure I was okay.

He lifts a shoulder. "I wanted to. And it's not exactly a sacrifice for me to get to spend the night on the couch with you."

"You say that now," I tease. "But that's because I haven't put on the movie yet."

Grabbing the vase of flowers, I move them to the coffee table so we can enjoy them from the couch, and Landon follows behind with our cupcake plate and forks.

"Do you want wine?" he asks.

"Sorry, I don't have any," I say, sinking into my usual spot on the couch.

Landon smiles, then turns back to the kitchen, reappearing with a bottle of cabernet in hand. "You think I didn't come prepared?"

I grin, moving to get up and help him uncork it, but he holds out a hand to stop me.

"I've got it. You get comfy. I'll find what I need."

I settle a bit deeper into my groove in the cushions. "If you insist."

Once we're snuggled up under the blanket with wine in hand, I reach for the remote and press **PLAY**. The familiar intro music sends chills up my arms, and I do a little happy dance in my seat.

Landon laughs, winding one arm around my waist and tugging me closer to him. "You're not going to sing along, are you?"

I shoot him a devious grin. "Would that annoy you?"

"Yes."

"Then yes," I say with a firm nod. "Yes, I will."

The movie isn't long, but it goes by even quicker when I'm looking over at Landon every other minute, watching for his reaction. He holds me a little extra tight during the sad songs, and when I give a rousing rendition of "Tomorrow," he applauds at the end, laughing like crazy. To top it all, when Annie finds out the truth about the people claiming to be her parents, I swear I see tears forming in his eyes.

"Damn flowers," he mumbles, wiping his eyes with the back of his hand. "I think I'm allergic."

I snuggle up a little closer to him, resting my cheek on his shoulder. "Whatever you say."

Once the movie is over and the credits are rolling, I push back from him just enough to look him in the eye. "Well?"

"Awful movie. Absolutely horrible," he says with conviction. But that tone can't disguise the flush that's still lingering on his cheeks and the sappy smile he wore when I sang along.

"Uh-huh." I give him a knowing look, crooking one finger to beckon him closer. "Get over here, tough guy. I know it got to you."

He's mindful of my shoulder as he pulls me into him again, pressing a kiss against my temple.

"I didn't bring it up for the whole movie, so I have to ask now. How's your shoulder?"

I roll my eyes. "I told you, it's fine. I'll have the results in a week."

"And you'll call me as soon as you know."

"Sure."

"And you'll tell me if anything pops up like this again so I can drive you."

"Yes, sir." I scoff, giving him a sharp salute.

His eyes narrow into serious slits. "Don't tease me. Let me worry about you."

"You don't have to, you know? I'm a big girl. I can handle it."

"I know that. I like that you're a strong woman, believe me. It's one of the things that attracted me to you, and something I definitely want in a partner."

I chew on my lower lip, weighing his words.

"I travel a lot during the year when the season starts. So a relationship with someone needy or codependent would never work for me. I want an equal. A strong woman who's going to miss me, sure, but who can take care of herself when I'm away. But that doesn't mean I don't want to take care of you too, Aubree. I do. Let me."

"I'll try." The words feel tight in my throat.

God, where did this man come from? I've been on my own for so long, telling myself I don't need anyone else. But now he's here, so strong and solid, and he smells so good, and there's just something about him—his words, his soothing presence—that I can't deny.

He's growing on me.

Like a suspicious mole.

CHAPTER TEN

Asking for a Friend

Landon

"What are we drinking tonight, boys?" Justin asks as I settle into the back corner of the booth, which, as everyone knows is the absolute worst seat, and the reason it's been reserved for me as the rookie on the team. Whoever occupies it is completely out of luck if he needs to get out to, say, use the restroom or make a private phone call, since he'd have to climb over four hockey players to do so.

"I'm down with whatever," I say.

I'm out with the guys from my team tonight. While they still like to give me a hard time about being the rookie, I'm grateful for the friendships I've formed. Teddy, Owen, and Asher helped me move into my new apartment last month, and when it was my birthday, the entire crew took me out and got me good and drunk. So if it makes them feel better to stick me in the corner, I'll deal with it.

When the bright-eyed, bubbly server swings by—a young woman with an Australian accent whose nametag reads **RACHEL**—we order a couple of pitchers of beer. She lingers at our table for a few moments too long, her gaze jumping from the blue of my eyes, to Justin's broody smirk, then over to Teddy's mischievous grin. It seems the sight of us has rendered her momentarily speechless.

She does a double-take, her eyes making another greedy pass. As she takes in Asher's blond hair and easy smile, her lips part. Then her gaze drifts to Owen's broad chest, and she makes a small helpless noise of surprise.

I've seen this type of reaction before when we're all out together—women have checked us out, sure—but there's usually a hint of subtlety to it. This poor girl's eyes look like they're going to pop out of her head, and she doesn't seem even remotely capable of carrying out her job duties. She's still staring at Owen's bulky arms, which are now crossed in front of his chest.

I've seen him command this type of female attention before—many times, in fact—but this is the first time I've seen it bother him. Maybe it's because he's engaged to be married soon, or maybe because he just really wants a beer. Either way, his smile has faded.

I clear my throat, pulling her attention over to me again. "He's taken, sweetheart," I murmur gently.

Her face falls, and she stammers out an apology. "So sorry. I was staring, wasn't I? I'll be right back with those pitchers." She hustles away with a flourish, and the guys around me chuckle.

"Speaking of being taken," Justin says, raising his eyebrows and looking in my direction. "You still off the market, Covey, or did you and Aubree get that shit taken care of?"

"Uh, we're still married, if that's what you're asking."

Owen scoffs, laughing. "Dude, but why? Surely there were easier ways to get into her panties than putting a ring on it."

Teddy chuckles into his fist.

"Yeah, what's the story?" Asher asks, his brows pushed together as he studies me. "How complicated is the annulment process? You don't have to go back to the great state of Nevada, do you?"

I'm not sure how much to share with them. On one hand, it's private, my personal business with Aubree, and I don't particularly feel like airing it. But on the other hand, these guys are my bros, the only family I have in this city, and they're bound to find out sooner or later anyway.

"Spill it, rookie," Justin says, eyeing me from across the table.

I shift uncomfortably. "I might want to, I don't know, see where this goes between me and Aubree."

"Wait. Hold the fuck up. What are you saying?" Owen asks, shaking his head in disbelief. "You're going to stay married?"

"I don't know, but yeah. I guess what I'm saying is before I agree to a divorce, shouldn't I at least date my wife?"

After these words leave my mouth, there's nothing but silence—dead-to-the-world, no-one's-even-breathing silence. And, yeah, I know what I've just told them is a little crazy. But with the slack-jawed, wide-eyed looks the guys are giving me, you'd think I just told them I'm an alien on a deep space mission sent to anally probe them.

Then Owen opens his mouth to say, "Plot twist!" and laughs under his breath.

After several more beats of uncomfortable silence, Justin says, "That's just fucking cr—"

But I hold up one hand, stopping him as I bark out, "You know what? It's not a big deal, and I'm not looking for opinions."

"Hey, you don't owe us an explanation," Asher says with a trace of sympathy, palms up.

"And Aubree is a cool girl," Teddy adds, nodding.

I nod once, grunting.

Fuck, why is this so awkward? And of course my choice of seating makes it impossible to escape. I just have to sit here and endure their loud stares and stony silence. *Fantastic.*

Our waitress chooses this moment to appear beside our table. She's bright pink when she returns with two pitchers of IPA and half a dozen glasses.

"Thank you, Rachel." I smile at her, and she lets out a choked gasp. This poor girl's discomfort shouldn't distract me from my own, but . . . well, it does. And I'll take whatever distraction I can get.

I let out a slow exhale and accept the glass of beer Asher's just poured me.

"We could slip her Grant's number," Teddy says with a snicker as she scurries away again.

"Yeah, and he'd kick all our asses," Asher says.

"Fact," I say, agreeing.

Our team captain, Grant, is the one person on the team I can't seem to figure out. He rarely ventures out with us, and when he does, he's a grumpy bastard. Go figure. I certainly don't want to get on the dude's bad side.

"You should've seen him at rookie camp last year. I thought he was going to murder Morgan," Justin says, launching into a story that involves a prank that went south.

Since the conversation has turned to hockey, and off my love life, I take a large gulp of beer, hoping it quenches whatever this weird tight feeling is inside my chest.

By the time I make it back to my place, I'm no more settled than I was sitting in that damn booth, enduring the awkward stares of my teammates. But Teddy was right, Aubree is a cool girl—and she's also sweet and funny and unbelievably freaking gorgeous.

This just makes sense, right? Dating until we can figure out this thing between us? Or maybe that's just another lie I tell myself, like *I'm only staying for one beer*. I had three, for the record.

I go through my bedtime routine on autopilot. Removing my contacts. Brushing my teeth. Stripping out of my jeans and T-shirt and throwing them in the hamper inside my closet. But by the time I fall into bed, I'm nowhere near ready for sleep, because my mind is still spinning on what-ifs.

Everything is jacked right now. From my empty bed to my naked ring finger, to the ridiculous luxury SUV that taunts me from the parking garage every day. Yes, I like Aubree a lot, but who the hell knows what will happen? She says she's trying, but she's holding herself back. She wasn't even going to tell me about her little surgical procedure. I'm really not sure what to make of that.

I roll onto my back and stare up at the ceiling as I release a slow sigh. I consider jerking off, wondering if maybe that will relax me. But somehow, I know it won't satisfy the ache inside me.

CHAPTER ELEVEN

Once a Pro, Always a Pro

Aubree

"**Y**ou have to at least give me a hint."

It's Friday night, and I'm riding beside Landon in his car, scanning my surroundings for any hints of our destination.

"No way." He shakes his head, his resolve firm. "You've made it this long without knowing. What's a few more minutes?"

His masculine, woodsy scent fills the small space between us, and I inhale deeply, nervous excitement bubbling inside me.

"One clue." I beg shamelessly, batting my eyelashes at him.

His chest rises and falls with a deep breath, and when we stop at a red light, his blue eyes fix on mine. "Why are you so interested? You've barely agreed to date me . . ."

"That's not true, is it?"

His smile is strained. "I don't know. You tell me, Aubree."

The sound of my name on his lips makes my heart stutter. The last time we were together at my place, he was so sweet. And when I called him to tell him the biopsy results from the mole I had removed came back as nothing, he was elated. It was cute.

"I'm here because I want to be," I say, darting another glance his way.

His thumb moves across his lower lip, and he gazes out at the road again. "Good. That's a start, I suppose."

I keep my expression neutral, hoping he doesn't know about the nerves that dance down my spine. Being near him makes me feel off-kilter. When we're apart, it's easy to tell myself I don't feel anything for him. But in his presence, that's just not possible. He affects me, plain and simple.

I smile, pretending I've not been split into a million fragmented pieces. My own feelings aren't something I'm used to struggling with. But on the matter of my hot new husband, they totally are.

"Fine." He sounds annoyed, but his slight smile tells me otherwise. "Here's your clue. Since you still seem hung up on our age difference, I thought we should do something to make us both feel young again."

We roll to a stop at a red light, and I scan the bars and restaurants around us. "Are we doing tequila shots and karaoke?" I ask, sizing up the karaoke bar on our right. "Because that pretty much sums up my college experience."

Landon chuckles, speeding past the bar the second the light turns green. "I said it'll make us feel young, not nauseous. Think a little bit younger."

I chew on my lower lip, turning the clock back a few more years. "We aren't going to be babysitting, are we?"

His full-body laugh reverberates through me. "No more guesses. We're just about there."

A mile or two later, a giant complex emerges in the distance. I can see the words FAMILY FUN ZONE glowing in blue neon lights.

"Is that where we're heading?"

"Bingo."

As we pull into the parking lot, I count one minivan to every three youngsters sprinting across the blacktop, most of them waving fistfuls of tickets or carrying cheaply made stuffed animals.

"Are we legally allowed in a place like this without kids?"

He shakes his head at me before swinging open his car door to hop out. "Don't worry, I called ahead. Adults like laser tag and arcade games too, you know."

With my hand in his, we walk through the parking lot and up to the oversize doors with the words THIS WAY TO FUN! printed in big, goofy lettering on the front. One step inside, and we're immediately met with that familiar arcade smell, a mixture of cheap pizza and socks. It's as gross as it is weirdly comforting.

Landon was right. I already feel like a kid again.

"Where to first? The Family Fun Zone is our oyster." He spreads his arms wide across the room of arcade games, and my eyes lock on two Skee-Ball machines near the back.

"Are you down for some Skee-Ball? I was

practically a pro when I was twelve."

He nods, pulling his wallet from his back pocket. "I'm game."

We find a token kiosk, and Landon feeds it a twenty, filling a plastic cup to the brim with quarter-size gold coins. "This should last us a few rounds."

"All I need is one round to kick your ass," I tease, then instantly clap a hand over my mouth when I remember the word *family* is literally in the name of this place. "I mean, to kick your heinie."

Landon chuckles as he passes the cup off to me. "I thought I'd escaped the horrors of that word."

We maneuver through the maze of arcade games to the back, squaring up to a Skee-Ball machine. Two tokens bring it to life, causing the lights to flash and six balls to pour into the chamber.

Landon grabs one, turning it over in his hand. "I'm not used to games with balls. I'm more of a puck guy."

"Well, what the puck are you waiting for?" I squeeze his side playfully, and he flinches, holding back a smile.

Note to self: My husband is ticklish. That may be useful info to have in the future.

The childlike joy in Landon's eyes disappears for a moment, replaced by a look of pure concentration as he lines up his first ball and rolls it up the alley. It hits the cage with a clatter and comes flying back at him.

"Shit," he mumbles under his breath, but I can barely hear it over my laughter. His gaze sweeps from the blank scoreboard over to me. "This is harder than I thought."

I hold out a hand, wiggling my fingers until he places the ball in my palm. Finding my stance, I focus my eyes on the prize and roll. *Boom*. Five hundred points.

His eyes narrow, skeptical. "Are you sure you haven't played since you were twelve?"

I shrug, picking up a second ball and rolling it straight into the center target. "Once a pro, always a pro, I guess."

With a laugh, he tugs me close to him, pressing a kiss to the top of my head and giving my ass a quick squeeze that's hardly appropriate for a family-friendly arcade. "Well then, show me how it's done, pro."

I shamelessly use the excuse of teaching Landon how to play as an opportunity to hang on to his muscular arms, moving him through the best technique. The games fly by, and before long, our fingertips hit the bottom of the token cup. I let him take the last game, and when he finally sinks a ball into the 200-level target, I cheer like he just scored a game-winning goal. And by the way he's beaming with pride, you'd think that's exactly what just happened.

"Care to celebrate with some crappy pizza?" I ask, tilting my head toward the snack bar.

"How about we get out of here and I buy you some *good* pizza?"

"Deal." I tear off the lengthy roll of tickets we earned and hand them off to a cute little girl waiting her turn at the racing game before following Landon out the door.

The place he has in mind, it turns out, is a cozy little wood-fired pizza place down the street. The hostess seats us right away, and without even looking at the menu, Landon orders for both of us—one Greek flatbread and one with prosciutto.

"I take it you've been here before," I say, grabbing a slice of bread from the basket between us before nudging it toward him.

He nods, snagging a roll. "A bunch of us took

Asher's niece to play laser tag when his family was in town. We ate here after."

"I didn't know you got to meet Asher's family."

"Just a few of them. His family is enormous. You should meet his niece Fable. She's a little spit-fire, like a tiny version of you."

"Oh?" I tilt my head, a smile creeping across my lips. "Are you calling me a spitfire?"

He holds up one finger as he finishes chewing. "Sure am. It's one of the things I like most about you. Apart from your Skee-Ball skills, that is."

"Oh, really? Is that all?" I ask, leaning in a little closer.

His eyes darken, and he licks his lips. "I like your ass a lot too, especially the way it looks in leggings. But my favorite thing is the way you sound when you come."

My cheeks flush with heat, but I don't look away from him. "Are you ever going to let me repay the favor?" I ask in a low voice, pulling my bottom lip between my teeth.

"Fuck yes. But only when you're ready, because we're doing this at your pace."

My heart stutters in my chest. "Landon . . ."

"I mean it."

Seriously, how is this man real?

By the time our pizzas arrive, Landon has already made me almost choke on my bread from laughing three separate times—all from stories involving the hockey guys taking Fable to the Family Fun Zone.

"I swear it, we didn't let her win," he says with a laugh, holding his right hand in the air. "She's just actually that good at laser tag. But I don't think Owen will ever live down scoring zero points."

"I can't believe this is the first I'm hearing of this." I pull a piece of prosciutto pizza from the plate, helping myself to a hearty bite. Landon was right to take the reins on ordering. This is freaking delicious.

"Owen made us promise not to bring it up, but I have reason to believe Justin might be including it in his best man speech."

I laugh. "I didn't think it was possible, but I'm officially even more excited for that wedding now."

It's quiet for a moment as Landon drags a napkin across his lips, then takes a big gulp of water to wash down the four pieces of pizza he's already put away.

"Speaking of the wedding, can I, uh, assume that you'll be my date?" His eyes glisten at me from across the table, brimming with hope.

As unbelievable as this pizza is, I know without a doubt that the best part of this meal is his enormous smile when I say yes. I think Ana might be right. Either that, or she was just really good at bribing me via ramen noodles. Either way, my decision has been made. Maybe it's not such a bad idea to date my husband.

When our check comes, Landon swipes the bi-fold, tucks his credit card inside, and hands it back to the waitress. "So, where to next?"

I purse my lips, holding back the yawn I can feel coming on. "Am I lame if I say we should head home?"

"A little," he says, pinching his thumb and forefinger together to demonstrate the exact size of my lameness. "But no worries."

The waitress returns with Landon's card, and he adds a tip and then scribbles something that sort of resembles a signature on the receipt before pushing to his feet. "Ready to go?"

Although I'll never be ready for this night to end, I push to my feet and follow him back to the car.

Outside, the sun has barely set, leaving the sky a gorgeous shade of purplish blue. The whole trip home feels like driving through a watercolor painting, right up to the moment Landon stops in front of my building, his hand moving from my thigh to the gearshift to put the car in park.

I'm almost embarrassed by how much I miss his touch the second he pulls away. Yes, I'm sleepy. But being in a family-friendly environment for most of the evening means I haven't so much as kissed Landon tonight. And I think we need to fix that.

"You can come in, if you want." I try to make it sound like a casual suggestion, even when every inch of my skin is practically begging for him to get his hands back on me.

Landon's thick brows push together as he studies me. "It's your apartment, Bree. It's not about what I want."

He's right, so I say, "Let me try that again. I want you to come inside."

His perfect, plush lips form a crooked smile

that just barely hints at his adorable dimple. "Then I'd love to."

He hops out of the car and crosses around the front to open my door for me. It's the kind of thing I'd normally put up a fight about, but I'm trying to be better about letting him take care of me in little ways.

We both seem to hold our breath as I fumble with the keys. Finally, I manage to get the door unlocked and lead us inside. Once the door closes behind us, Landon lifts my chin toward his, claiming my mouth with a passionate kiss.

The air around us feels heavy with expectation, and when I pull back and meet his gaze, my stomach clenches at what I see reflected back at me. There's so much need brimming in his dark blue eyes.

Something is changing between us, and I'm not sure what to make of that. He's opened himself up, shared personal details that I doubt many others know. And coupled with his intense interest in me, in *us,* it's making me soften, making me feel things I didn't expect.

I press my hands into his firm, wide chest, my fingers gripping his T-shirt. Lifting up on my toes again, I fasten my mouth to his in another slow kiss.

"Fuck," he growls against my lips. "Been waiting to kiss you all night."

He's looking at me like he wants to devour me. There's just one thing standing in his way. An insane amount of restraint. And even that is sexy as hell.

"Bedroom?" I whisper against his chest, my fingers still gripping his shirt.

Without a word, Landon scoops me up in his arms. My legs tighten around his waist as my lips trail over the rough column of his throat. He carries me a few steps, then stops in his tracks.

"What's wrong?" I ask, my chest suddenly tight.

The slightest bit of pink creeps across his stubbled cheeks. "I, uh, don't know where your bedroom is."

My bubble of laughter mixes with his rumbly one in the most beautiful harmony I've ever heard. How did I forget that this is only his second time here?

"Down the hall to the left," I manage to say through my giggles. "The room with the bed."

With big, hurried strides, Landon carries me to my room, lays me gently across my duvet, and sinks down beside me. With all the patience in the world, he runs his palm along the length of my thigh. He brushes his fingers over the front of my jeans, and I jolt. His tender touches are going to be my demise. Resisting him is futile. Pointless.

When I press my hand over his zipper, Landon curses softly. His breath against my neck is deep, but rapid, and I attack his mouth with mine. He tries to slow the kiss down, to draw things out, but I'm having none of that. My pulse riots, and heat tears through my veins like wildfire. I want him. Need him.

When I caress the firm bulge in the front of his jeans again, Landon makes a breathless sound.

"Aubree . . ." He says my name like a warning.

We're going too far. In over our heads. But I'm powerless to stop it.

Uncertainty swims in his blue gaze. His control is hanging by a thread, and I want to see it snap.

Lust fills his features, and *dear God*, if I thought he was attractive before, this is flat-out unfair.

"Why does this feel so good?" I say on a groan,

my eyes meeting his hooded ones.

"This is all I've ever wanted," he murmurs, the rough pads of his fingers touching my cheek. Even though he doesn't say it with words, I can see the question reflected back at me.

Why can't it be me and you in the end?

Heat rushes through me like a tidal wave, washing away all logical thought.

His eyes are desperate. I have no idea why this matters to him so much, but it obviously does.

My body wants him. My brain thinks this is crazy. My heart isn't sure.

But when Landon slides his palm up my calf, my body wins out.

With deft fingers, he opens the button of my jeans and tugs them to the floor. And when he discovers that my panties are wet, his groan is filled with deep satisfaction.

"Good God, baby." His fingers trail along the damp scrap of black lace, leaving me twitching. "So wet for me already."

With a quick tug, my panties join my jeans on the floor, and his palms press against my inner thighs, which I ease apart. I feel so exposed, so plainly on display for him like this, and for a minute, I wish I'd turned off the lights. But then he levels himself with my center, breathing me in as he slides two thick fingers into my heat, and I know for sure that nothing has ever felt as good as this.

Gradually, he moves faster, crooking his fingers inside me to hit a softer, deeper spot. Just when I'm positive this couldn't get any more heavenly, he brings his tongue to my center, sending a jolt of pure electricity through me. My hips buck with need, every stroke of his tongue bringing me closer and closer to climax.

"Landon, please." I beg shamelessly, digging my nails into his shoulders as I teeter on the edge for a long, breathless moment. "I'm so close."

He groans in approval against me, and in that moment, I completely let go. With one last desperate sigh, I freefall into him, tumbling harder and faster than ever before.

It takes a good, long moment for me to catch my breath. He is undeniably good at that. When he rises to his feet, he towers over me, and my eyes instantly lock on the erection pressing into the front of his jeans.

Propping myself up onto my elbows, I reach out one curious hand, stroking him through the denim. His eyes flutter closed, a low, satisfied hum building in his throat.

"Okay?" I blink up at him, enjoying the look of pleasure on his face.

"God, yes." His voice is low and thick with an edge of barely restrained desire. It's irresistible. All of him is.

With eager fingers, I unbutton his jeans, holding my breath a little as I shift his boxers out of the way to free his length.

Holy. Shit.

He's huge.

If ever there was such a thing as a beautiful cock, this is it. Smooth, curving up ever so slightly. And what this man lacks in age, he makes up for in inches. I want to take my time with him, stroking and tasting every inch.

But not tonight. Tonight, I just want to make him come for me. He's been so patient, after all.

Once Landon is free from his jeans and the black cotton boxers, he joins me on the bed, touching my shoulder, stroking my collarbone, kissing my neck as I curl my fingers around him. With a steady grip, my hand slides up and down his thick erection in long strokes. I can hear his heartbeat thumping inside his chest as he sucks in one shaky breath after another, watching me with hungry eyes as I move a little faster.

"Just like that, baby." He tenses and twitches beneath my touch, his chest rising as he inhales. "Just like that. You're gonna make me come."

My eyes narrow, a sultry smile twitching on my lips as I watch his control start to waver. His hips thrust into my fist in uneven jerks. "Come for me, Landon."

As if on command, he steadies one hand on my hip and lets go, jetting across my stomach in wet, hot bursts.

It's quiet for a moment as his breathing returns to normal, his eyes focused on the hand still pressed against the bed until he finally cuts through the silence with a soft exhale.

After pressing a thankful kiss into my forehead, he disappears into the bathroom, returning with toilet paper in excess to clean me up. "Sorry about this," he mutters, wiping up his mess.

"Don't be."

Once we're all cleaned up, I pull back my duvet, gesturing for him to crawl in with me. I don't know if he wants to spend the night or not, but no way is he bolting out of here after that.

I sigh, nestling in under the covers. "I missed this."

"What?" he asks, his voice harsh.

"Having a cuddle buddy."

He tugs me closer. "Then get your hot ass over here, sweetheart."

"You don't mind cuddling? I thought most guys hated it."

"That's not true, is it?" He breathes against my hair.

"I'm pretty sure it's a universally known fact. It's one of those things that's merely tolerated after sex." I shift, bringing us closer. "And you don't even get the benefit of that."

"Well, maybe I'm not most guys."

"Trust me, I figured that out."

His arms feel so good and so solid around me.

"I like cuddling with you too," he says after a

moment of comfortable silence. "Plus, I'm pretty sure it's in the husband job description somewhere, isn't it?"

I think he's kidding, but his words put a tiny knot of worry in my chest.

Is that all I am to him? An obligation? Something that he's trying to do the right thing by?

It's a thought that stings more than I thought it would.

• • •

Landon

Aubree seems to have let go of her insecurities about our age difference, and the last thing I want to do is set her off again, so I hope my question won't do that.

"Can I ask you something?" I ask, stretching to bring one arm around her in the bed.

She nods, picking at a piece of lint on the duvet. "Go for it."

"Why are you still single?"

She lifts her head from its resting spot on my chest and gives me an uncertain look. "What do you mean?"

I shrug. "You're obviously a catch. Smoking hot. Fun. Smart. Amazing at Skee-Ball."

She smirks. "Go on . . ."

I smile. "Well, I'm not going to lie and tell you that you're a good dancer. You're not, babe."

"Shush." She swats my arm. "Just ask me what you wanted to ask me."

"Well, I was just wondering why you haven't settled down with someone yet?"

She licks her lips, weighing my question. "I've dated a lot, but I always kept things casual. I guess it's just because I've always prioritized my job over my relationships. I love what I do, you know, and it's important work."

I nod. "That's a good reason, I guess."

She inhales, releasing the breath slowly as she lays her head back down against my chest. "Maybe. But I know you're right. If I don't want to end up old and alone, I'm going to need to learn to make room for a man in my life."

That's not what I asked, but I don't point that out. And since I'm hoping to be that man in her future, at her side, I don't want to press my luck. "Today was a good start."

She nods. "It was fun." There's a long pause before Aubree continues. "I haven't told you this before, but my parents divorced when I was young."

"How old were you?"

"Little. First grade, I think. I hardly remember a time when they were together, so the divorce itself wasn't difficult on me. But I watched my mom go from relationship to relationship, always looking for a man to fulfill her. I guess that left an impression."

I'm pleased that Aubree's finally letting me in, but I opt to stay quiet and just run my fingertips along her arm, hoping she'll continue. And after a little while, she does.

"I vowed that I would never be like that—dependent on a man with nothing for myself. I didn't want to repeat her mistakes. So I went to college, focusing on myself, my goals, my grades, applying for the best internships. I was driven, and I never really focused on dating. I liked that about myself, you know? I took pride in that."

"And you should."

I want to ask if she feels differently now. Even if I do respect the hell out of her for creating the future she wants for herself, I hope she's starting to consider how I might fit into that future too. But am I brave enough to ask her?

Nope.

Instead, I just enjoyed the feel of her in my arms, and try to quiet the worry in my head.

CHAPTER TWELVE

Relationship Goals

Landon

It's Saturday night, and we're all at Justin and Elise's penthouse apartment.

There's pizza and beer, and the basketball playoffs are on TV, though no one's really watching it because everyone is clustered into small groups engaged in low conversation. Aubree is outside on the balcony with the ladies, enjoying the early evening breeze, while I'm inside with the guys, camped out around the kitchen counter, or more importantly, around the food.

She and I didn't arrive together, and when I got here, I greeted her with a hug and a kiss pressed to her cheek. The strange looks and gasps from our friends were hard to ignore, but exactly what I did. Because whatever this is between Aubree and me, it's no one's business but ours.

"How's wedding planning coming?" Teddy asks Owen around a mouthful of pizza.

"Straight. Everything's done now. We're just waiting for the RSVP cards to roll in." Owen gives everyone a pointed look and waves his finger. "Which means, don't forget to send those in."

"I'll be there," Asher says. "Count me in."

Owen shakes his head. "Dude, don't *tell* me. Just send in the damn card. My mom loves collecting those little fuckers from the mailbox each day, and she calls Becca every night with a tally. There are seating charts, and yeah, basically it's a whole *thing*."

Asher nods, looking a bit panicked. I'd bet a hundred bucks that he already threw the card away. "Fine. I'll send in the damn card," he mutters, his eyes narrowed.

"You ready to be tied down to one woman for all of eternity?" Jordie asks, smirking.

"Hell yeah, man. I can't wait," Owen says, grinning like the lovesick fool he is.

Based on Jordie's shocked expression, he was expecting a different response, for Owen to groan or laugh off the comment.

Even if I wouldn't admit it to him, it's actually pretty awesome how devoted he and his fiancée Becca are to each other. Hashtag relationship goals and all that.

I help myself to another bottle of beer and can't help but think about how confusing things have been with Aubree. I bought her a car. Asked her to move in with me. Aren't those the kind of things a good boyfriend does?

"Any tips on how to keep your woman happy? I'm all ears, boys," I say with what I hope is an easygoing chuckle. But it comes out as more of a strained laugh, because is Aubree really my woman?

Owen grins. "You know what usually does the trick when Becca's mad at me about something?"

Suddenly, I'm a little worried about what's going to come flying out of his mouth next. Although I hope it's something helpful, because I really need to gain some useful knowledge in Wife Management 101, I'm thinking his comment probably isn't going to help at all.

"What's that? I ask nervously.

"A good smash session," he blurts out, plopping down onto a stool at the kitchen counter.

I roll my eyes. "Right, yeah, let me just make note of that."

"I'm serious, dude," Owen says. "Sex releases all kinds of endorphins. It's science. Look it up." He points to my phone lying facedown on the counter as he says this. "Plus, it feels really fucking good."

"That's the least helpful thing I've ever heard," I say dryly.

He grins. "It's hard to stay angry when you feel amazing."

Teddy and Asher nod like this is actually sound advice. They're such dumbasses. Sometimes I wonder how I'm the youngest member of this group.

"No, I meant it's not helpful because I've haven't done that."

Owen's eyebrows push together. "Wait. With Aubree or with anyone?"

"Can we just drop this?" I mutter. It's not really the conversation I intended on having tonight. And certainly not with my teammates.

"Hell no, we can't." Owen leans forward on his

elbows, his gaze meeting mine. "So you've never fucked? Like, ever?" His voice is filled with wonder and confusion.

I take a deep breath, trying to calm down. Owen's about as subtle as a brick to the face.

"No," I say flatly.

"In your whole life?" He blinks, staring at me in wonderment. "Like never?"

"Last time I checked."

"Jesus, dude." Owen shudders like the thought of abstaining physically pains him. "How have you survived?"

"I'm not a monk. I've been with girls. Just haven't checked that particular item off the list yet."

"Why the fuck not?" Owen's face is drawn tight.

"Owen, drop it." Asher chides him, giving me a sympathetic look. "Leave the guy alone. It's his decision."

I swallow. "It's fine, Ashe." I wave him off, perfectly able to fight my own battles. "Because I was waiting for the right girl."

Jordie's eyes are wide, and even Teddy has a shocked expression.

"Oh." Owen breathes out the word on an exhale like he still can't quite believe it.

I guess I get it. I mean, pussy is thrown around so often. Girls are always readily available to us, even to the guys on the team who are missing half their damn teeth. And before he got engaged, Owen was the kind of guy who indulged in it regularly, so his shock doesn't surprise me, even if it is a little annoying.

"Let's just move on, okay?"

Owen holds up one hand. "Of course. I'm sorry if I sounded like an asshole. I'm in full support of whatever you and your dick want to do—or don't want to do."

This pulls a laugh out of me, despite my surly mood.

I half expect him to demand to be the first to know when I finally give in and give it to Aubree, but thankfully he doesn't.

"No means no," Teddy says, raising his beer to me in a silent toast.

God, my friends are idiots.

Aubree chooses that moment to come inside from the balcony where she's been chatting with the girls. Her hair is down, loose around her shoulders in soft waves, and she looks gorgeous. Memories of our last night together crash through me.

She tosses a flirty look my way, her eyes meeting mine with mischief, her lips parted with the hint of a smile. It's the same kind of look she might make if she was in my lap riding my cock. My dick doesn't fail to notice, hardening against my thigh without my permission.

I should feel like a shit for objectifying her. But who could blame me? My wife is hot as sin. Curves. Sass. Intelligence. She's got it all.

My brain takes a sharp detour into the gutter, and I'm powerless to stop it. I shift my restless cock against my thigh, hoping I can get through the rest of the night without a string of filthy thoughts running rampant through my head.

We may not have come to the party together, but I'm going to make damn sure we leave it together.

CHAPTER THIRTEEN

Boy Toy

Aubree

Summer nights in Seattle don't get much better than this. The breeze is gentle, the sun has just set, and for the first night in what feels like forever, all the girls are together. We're lounging on the wicker patio furniture on Owen and Becca's balcony, sipping beer and catching up on each other's summers. It's the kind of night that makes me wish I didn't have the thought of leaving this city in just a few short months hanging over my head.

Elise mouths the words *Are you okay?* at me from across the balcony, and I nod, managing a smile.

I made the mistake of checking my work email today, something I normally try to avoid on weekends, and my mind hasn't stopped wandering to the promotion my boss offered me since. It's making it hard to just be present and enjoy this perfect, rare moment when it's just us girls.

I shift in my seat, refocusing my attention on the conversation. How many nights like this do I have left before I leave?

Becca must be able to read minds or something, because seemingly out of the blue, she steers the conversation toward me. "How's work been for you, Bree?"

"Same old, same old," I lie, mindlessly picking the label off my second beer of the evening. I haven't yet shared with my friends the slightly life-changing information that I won't be living in Seattle much longer. Actually, I haven't told anyone, unless you count my landlord when I failed to renew the apartment I'm living in for next year.

"Any big fundraising events coming up?" she asks.

I just shake my head. "Just meetings on top of meetings." That part isn't a lie. I'm just leaving out the exact details of said meetings.

The conversation veers toward a more interesting subject, Sara and Teddy's recent trip to the Virgin Islands. As Sara recounts the details of snorkeling next to sea turtles, I nod along, throwing in the occasional *Wow* and *Really?* at the appropriate times.

But mentally, I'm in the midst of a panic spiral, playing out worst-case scenarios of how everyone will react when I break the news. My friends will be sad, of course, but proud of me. They know how much I love my job, and this opportunity is too good to pass up.

But what about Landon?

I've been ignoring the guilt pressing down on my chest anytime he mentions the future. But how much longer can I go on pretending that I'm not on a limited timeline here in Seattle? And what does that mean for our relationship?

Becca lets out a dramatic gasp, and I snap my head toward her, convinced this time that she actually can read minds. But it looks like the source of the shock is on her phone, which her wide eyes are locked on.

"Sorry to interrupt, Sara." She gives our friend a quick apologetic look, then turns her head my way. "Bree, is Landon a virgin?"

My stomach does a backflip as everyone looks toward me expectantly. *Oh, joy.* The other secret

I've been keeping from my friends.

"Um . . ." I swallow. "Who told you?"

"Owen. Landon just told the guys." Becca taps one pink manicured nail against her phone screen.

"And he already texted you?"

Her smile is proud, maybe even a little smug. "We tell each other everything."

"Everything?" A challenging grin twitches across my lips. "Did he tell you about the time he lost in laser tag to a six-year-old girl?"

"No changing the subject," Sara says, wagging a finger, going total lawyer-mode on me. "Confirm or deny—Lovey still has his V-card."

I sigh. Now that it's out in the open, there's no use lying. "Confirm."

Before I can get in another word, my friends launch into a full-blown freak-out, gasping and chattering loud enough to warrant a noise complaint from the neighbors. You'd think I told them that my husband is from outer space.

"Why didn't you tell us?" Sara asks, her voice as sharp as I imagine it is in the courtroom.

"It didn't seem like my information to give out.

It's not really the kind of thing I could blurt out over brunch. *Oh, these eggs taste good. And, by the way, my husband is a virgin.*"

"Fair, fair." Bailey nods.

"But you've done, like, *other stuff*, right?" Becca's tone is one of genuine concern.

"Don't worry. He's a virgin, not a prude. And the fact that he hasn't officially done the deed means he's really good at, ahem, *other stuff*." I break out the air quotes, which gets a laugh.

"Cheers to that." Bailey tips her bottle toward me. "You're going to rock that boy's world."

"Don't I know it," I mumble, my mind wandering toward the surprise I have waiting for him in my bedside drawer. I really freaking hope he comes home with me tonight.

Sara sighs, leaning back in her chair. "I remember my first time. Senior year of high school on the couch in Christian Simmons's basement. He finished in about five seconds and then had the audacity to ask if I came."

Becca laughs so hard, she snorts. "If you have to ask, you already know the answer, buddy."

"At least you had a couch to work with," Bailey

190 | KENDALL RYAN

says. "My first time was in the back of my college boyfriend's car. His roommate was a total hermit and never left their dorm, so we had to get creative. I'm almost positive my statistics professor saw us."

"You didn't drive off campus?" Sara asks.

Bailey shakes her head. "Nope. Right on campus, and in broad daylight. What can I say? We were young, dumb, and horny."

Elise holds her hands up, palms out. "No awkward first-time stories from me. I've only been with Justin."

"You guys are so cute, it's borderline disgusting," Bailey says with a playful eye roll. "What about you, Aubree? How was your first time?"

"I hardly remember. That was freshman year of college. Over ten years ago." I visibly cringe at that number. *Ten freaking years. Damn, I feel old.* "Can we talk about something else, please?"

"Okay, new subject," Elise says, shifting in her seat. "Has anyone here taken a guy's V-card before?"

"Oh my God, that's the same subject!" I throw my arms up, spilling a bit of my beer.

"No, it's not. It's totally different!" Elise's gaze

flicks toward the sliding glass door. The guys have moved from the kitchen to the couch to watch the last few minutes of the game. "Well? Have any of you?"

Becca, Sara, and I all shake our heads, but Bailey is silent on the subject, grinning sheepishly from behind her beer.

Suspicious, I squint at her. "Bailey?"

"I've, uh . . . slept with three."

"Damn!" Becca laughs, breaking into a slow clap.

I lift my bottle and clink it with Bailey's. "I didn't know I was friends with the virgin-whisperer. Teach me your ways, oh wise one."

She drains what's left of her beer, setting it on the glass table before launching into a full-on TED Talk on the subject. "First of all, don't expect him to last very long. So, load up on foreplay if you want to get off. Which, like, of course you do. But for the most part, it's not going to be about you. It's about making it special and meaningful for him. Especially since he's waited for so long."

"Don't worry too much, okay?" Sara gives my arm a squeeze. "It's going to be fine. And then the second time, it's going to be, like, infinitely better."

Our conversation is interrupted by loud, enthusiastic cheers from inside, accompanied by the sound of someone being thumped on the back. The basketball game must be over, and from the sound of it, it ended well.

"Maybe we should head in," I say, tilting my head toward the sliding glass door. "It's getting chilly out here."

"Okay, but I just have one more question," Becca says, drumming her fingers against the bottle in her hand. "What's this about Owen losing at laser tag to a six-year-old?"

I smile, remembering what Landon said about Justin's best man speech. "Don't worry. I think you'll hear all about it at your wedding."

As we filter inside, the good-byes begin, and it isn't long before I feel a muscular arm sliding around my waist.

Landon's blue eyes darken as they lock with mine. "Any plans for the rest of the evening?" His voice is a low growl, and it lights a fire in my belly.

"I think I'm looking at them," I murmur, running my thumb along the hem of his worn Hawks tee. "My place?"

His keys jingle as he snatches them from his back pocket. "Meet you there."

"Deal."

Maybe Landon will get his world rocked sooner than I expected.

• • •

Back at my apartment, we head straight for the bedroom, tumbling onto my duvet as we crash into each other. His mouth finds mine in one hungry kiss after another, his tongue intertwining with mine in confident strokes.

I moan against his lips, dragging my nails down the muscular terrain of his back. Within moments, he's pulling his shirt over his head, discarding it on the floor before making quick work of mine.

His chest is so delicious that I actually sigh into his next kiss. My fingertips explore his wide pec muscles before trailing lower over the defined grooves etched into his abs. I press one hand against his jeans, enjoying the eager kick behind his zipper. Maybe it's time to show him the surprise I have in store.

With one hand still resting on the ridge in his jeans, I blink up at him eagerly. "I got you something."

Excitement flickers in his eyes. "A present?"

"Sort of. A toy."

His brows scrunch together. "What kind of toy?"

"You know, a *toy*."

I pull back from him, pressing a kiss against his stubbled jaw before reaching for my nightstand, tugging open the drawer, and pulling out the plastic box. Inside is a black silicone object with a soft pink end. It looks convincingly like a flashlight, which is the point, from what I understand.

"Ta-da." I set it down on the duvet in front of us, waiting for Landon to pick it up and unbox it.

Instead, he just stares, his eyes wide with either confusion or surprise, I can't quite tell.

"What the hell is that?"

"Come on. You know what it is." I give my eyebrows a flirty wiggle.

His expression stays blank, though, so maybe he actually doesn't know. "Is it . . . a sex toy?"

I smile encouragingly. "It is."

"But it's for, um, dudes," he says, his mouth now crooked with an amused grin.

"Yes. I thought it might be fun."

His gaze moves skeptically between my hand and the toy, then eventually meets mine. "Are you serious?"

I nod toward the box, giving him some much-needed encouragement. "Go ahead. Open it."

Slowly, he tears into the packaging, removes the toy, and tests it with a few curious pokes. My heart pounds out an uneven rhythm.

Hesitantly, he pushes one finger into the opening at the end, watching with curious eyes as it disappears into the silicone. "This feels pretty realistic," he admits, wiggling his finger around inside. I can hardly suppress my snicker.

I can't even tell you how nervous I was buying the dang thing. I ordered it online, and as soon as I hit **CONFIRM PURCHASE**, I was terrified that when they delivered the toy, it would be done by a van with the words **HOT SEX WAGON** emblazoned on the side, blasting the song "Me So Horny" through a loudspeaker mounted to the roof.

Of course, it wasn't anything as exciting as my overactive imagination had made it out to be. It came three days later in a plain brown box from a company with a name so boring, I've already forgotten what it was.

But now that we're sitting here, my idea to use it as an *intro* for him suddenly seems a little stupid. Until Landon smiles wickedly and pushes one hand into my hair, bringing his mouth close to mine.

"I kinda love that you bought this, even if I feel a little weird about the fact that I want to try it."

I smile and lean into his kiss. "Don't feel weird. It's going to be so hot watching you lose control."

He quirks one eyebrow at me.

"Wanna test it out?" I ask, grinning. Okay, I might be a little excited about this.

He pauses, turns the toy over in his hand, then nods, handing it to me. "Fuck yeah, but first you've gotta get naked, because there's no way tonight's going to be just about me."

With one more long, lingering kiss, Landon puts his fingers to work on the button to my jeans. When he slides his hand beneath the elastic of my panties, I give a little breathless groan.

"Landon . . ." I moan when he pushes one finger inside. "We need some lube."

His mouth lifts as he meets my eyes. "No, we don't."

"I meant—for, for the toy," I stammer.

"Oh, right."

He shifts to his feet to shove off his jeans and boxers, stepping out of them as he strokes himself once. He's already fully hard, and the sight of him in all his masculine glory makes my lower half clench.

I watch his hand as it absently glides up and down over his smooth shaft. Even though it's been only a day since I've had my hands on him, I'm desperate to feel him again. The moonlight illuminates his sculpted frame as he settles back onto the bed beside me, and it takes every bit of willpower in my body not to climb into his lap and sink down until every inch of him is inside me.

Patience, Aubree. That will come. One step at a time.

"Ready?" I add some of the lube I bought to the toy, then align the soft pink silicone with his swollen tip. When I turn to him for approval, he gives me a small sharp nod, and my heart throbs. *Here goes nothing.*

With a slow exhale, I push down, easing a few inches of him into the soft silicone opening. His eyes roll back in his head in response. *Oh hell, that's hot.*

"*Fuck,*" he curses, low under his breath.

"Yeah?" I give him another inch, earning me a desperate groan. A deep, throaty sound that makes my pulse race.

"God, yeah. That's unreal."

I press a kiss against his stubble, moving the toy a little farther down his shaft. "Just wait until you try the real thing."

A shudder courses through him as he shifts his hips forward, sinking another inch deeper. "Oh shit," he whispers as I pull the toy back toward his tip, then push back down, all the way to the base.

"Fuck, *fuck,*" he murmurs, his jaw clenched.

After that, he's speechless, reduced to short, shallow breaths as I work him over. A few more thrusts and those breaths turn to low, strained grunts.

It's way hotter than I ever imagined watching his wide chest rise with halting breaths, watching his fists clutch the sheets, listening to those deep pleasure-drenched sounds tumbling from his lips.

My body reacts immediately, tightening and growing needy for his touch. He's so insanely attractive. We kiss, and he touches my breasts, but he's obviously distracted, which is kind of adorable.

"Gonna come now." With one last sexy sound, he does, emptying himself in bursts as his chest heaves.

Holy hell, that was hot. I set the toy aside, waiting for him to regain his composure.

After a few shaky breaths, a satisfied smile breaks out on his face. "Jesus Christ. What do I owe you for that thing?"

A laugh falls from my lips as I run my fingers along the curve of his jaw. "You liked it?"

"Uh, yeah. In case you couldn't tell." His cheeks are slightly flushed, and he's still breathing hard.

"Well, I think I know of one way you can pay me back."

"Yeah?" His eyes turn a stormy dark blue as he wets his lower lip, tugging me to the edge of the bed and then sinking to his knees. "I think I can do that."

CHAPTER FOURTEEN

A First Time for Everything

Landon

"**C**heers," Teddy says, raising his glass of whiskey.

"You guys didn't need to do this. I already had a bachelor party," Owen says in protest, but he's grinning.

The truth is, summer will be over before we know it, and the rigors of training camp are mere weeks away. Which means this weekend is basically just an excuse to get drunk, eat badly, sleep in, and have bro-time. But, of course, it's all been done under the guise of a bachelor-party-bonding weekend with the groomsmen from Owen's wedding—Teddy, Asher, Justin, and me. His cousin Matt is in the wedding party too, I guess, but he lives in California and will only be coming into town for the wedding, which will take place in two weeks in Becca's hometown.

"Cheers," I say, and we all raise our glasses of expensive whiskey. It goes down smooth, and I can already tell my everything-in-moderation rule is going to be blown to shit tonight.

Not that I really mind.

We're staying here tonight in an old converted barn an hour north of the city. It's been turned into a luxury vacation rental, complete with vaulted ceilings and rustic hardwood floors, a clawfoot tub in the bathroom that I'm sure no one in this group will appreciate, and six bedrooms. Even if I get hammered, which is likely, based on the speed at which Teddy keeps refilling our glasses, all I have to do is make it up one flight of stairs and into the room with a queen-size bed that's mine for the next forty-eight hours.

"How are things going with you and Aubree?" Owen asks, his brows drawing together. "Still haven't smashed yet, I take it?"

I really wish I hadn't told him that. "We've been taking things slow, but yeah, things are good."

Good is an understatement, of course, but I can't tell him that, because this thing between Aubree and me is still fragile and a work in progress. Memories of our last night together—of the special gift she got me—send a flash of heat bolting down my spine. But our relationship is growing, and it's more than just the few sexy moments we've shared. I like being with her, a lot, and I find myself wanting to know every single thing about her.

Hoping to move the conversation along, I wander into the massive great room and plop down onto the L-shaped leather couch. Only I'm short on luck tonight, because the guys follow, Teddy grabbing the whiskey bottle from the kitchen counter before joining us. It's a testament to how massive this couch is that it can fit five hockey players comfortably.

"So, you guys haven't fucked yet, just to be clear?" Owen asks, abandoning all subtlety, and I glare at him.

"Have you been hit in the head with a puck too many times?"

"I remember my first time." Asher lets out a long sigh. "It was with a girl named Sarina in tenth grade. I thought I loved her."

"Tenth grade?" Teddy whistles low under his breath. "Mine wasn't until sophomore year of college."

Asher nods. "Yup. I thought I was a pretty big fucking deal. She was two years older than me. Although what happened after that kinda sucked."

Owen chuckles. "What … she spread rumors that you had a three-inch cock?"

"No, asshole." Asher heaves out a frustrated sound and grabs the bottle to refill his glass. "She broke my heart. Left me for some guy she met at Yale the following year. Although, if she could have spread any rumor, it would have been about my stamina. Because, yeah, it was over fast. Sixteen-year-old me had zero chill."

"Hey, Covey, you'd better start taking notes here," Teddy says. "Expect to last for about three pumps."

Justin shakes his head, leaning in to get into the conversation for the first time. "Not necessarily true. I was so nervous, I couldn't get there. It took almost an hour for me to finish."

"Thanks, guys." I hold up one hand. I'm not nearly drunk enough to be having this conversation with my teammates. "As much as I appreciate your advice, I think I'm good."

Owen has a faraway look in his eyes, like he's remembering something. Then he starts to chuckle. "Yeah, I forgot about that. I almost went soft when I put on the condom, because that fucker was so tight. So, yeah, you never know what might happen, Covington."

A frustrated groan pours out of me. "Dudes, with all due respect, shut the fuck up. Can we please talk about literally *anything* else?"

Unfortunately for me, they keep right on over-sharing.

I learn things I never, *ever* wanted to know about these dudes losing their V-cards. I mean, Asher cried after his first time, apparently. And Teddy proposed marriage. God, these cringe-worthy stories need to stop. *Immediately*.

"Hey, I'm just going to make a phone call," I say, rising to my feet. I don't wait for them to respond as I start down the hall. I didn't call Aubree when we arrived, and that seems like a very husbandly thing to do.

I slip into the hall bath and close the door, closing out the sound of their voices as I dial her number. She answers after the first ring.

"Hey. I missed you and wanted to hear your

voice," I say in greeting.

"Well, aren't you sweet?" I can tell she's smiling. "Are you having an amazing time?"

"I think I'm supposed to say yes, aren't I?"

She chuckles, and the sound of her laughter makes my own mouth quirk up.

"How was work? What are you doing?" I ask.

Aubree lets out a strained sigh. "Work is . . . a little complicated right now. But I'm good. Just hanging out at home tonight."

"I wish I was there with you. A quiet night in sounds perfect."

"So, what's wrong? You're not having fun?" she asks.

"They're drunk. And oversharing."

"The topic?"

"First times," I mutter, unamused.

"As in . . ."

"Yeah."

Aubree makes a breathless sound. "Oh, interesting. The girls might have done the same thing to me."

I chuckle. "You're kidding?"

"Nope. They ambushed me at Justin and Elise's place and started sharing details that I had absolutely no interest in learning."

My brows push together. *Sounds familiar.* "Why is everyone so obsessed with this?"

I hope she doesn't answer that question, because the topic of why my P hasn't been inside her V isn't one that's easily understood. It's like solving a complex mathematical equation. These things take time. Although, it's something that's been on my mind a lot lately.

"No clue," she says with a chuckle, saving me from some real embarrassment.

"Maybe we're not ready for primetime, but what about something a little more technology friendly?" I ask, my voice low.

"Phone sex?" Aubree murmurs, her voice lifting.

"I'm down if you are," I say, but all I can hear is her shallow breathing, and not much more. Maybe I've spooked her or pressed too hard.

"It's just . . . how would we even start?" she whispers.

I flip the lock on the bathroom door and lean one hip against the marble counter.

I could start by telling her I'm horny as fuck right now and trapped in a barn-turned-house with four other dudes. But somehow I don't think that would set the mood I'm going for. That mood being—how to get her fingers in her pussy so I can hear her moaning.

"Well . . ." I hesitate for just a second. "I could start by telling you that I haven't been able to stop thinking about that day in my apartment when I went down on you. You tasted so fucking good."

There's a sharp inhale of breath. "Are you alone right now?"

"Of course," I murmur. "I'm alone, and my dick is getting hard for you."

"Oh," she says on a groan. "That's a nice thought. Why don't you take it out for me?"

I exhale, my breath coming faster. "I might be able to do that. Where are you? Alone too?"

"I'm in my bed. Under the covers."

I draw down the zipper to my pants.

"Is that what I think it is?" she asks, slightly breathless.

"Maybe. First, slide your fingers under your shirt. Touch your perfect tits for me."

"Mmm. Done." She moans. "Tell me now."

I almost chuckle at her impatience, but I don't, because I wasn't kidding when I said I was hard for her. It's like all the blood in my body has been diverted to my sorely neglected dick.

"I'm taking my cock out. It's so hard for you, Aubree. What should I do?"

"Stroke it," she says.

"Wrapping it in my fist," I rasp out. "Put your fingers in your panties, baby."

"Already there," she whispers. "I'm wet."

A stuttered breath leaves my lungs, but I force the words out. "Good. Touch your clit for me while I jerk off."

She groans again, saying my name like it's a plea. I love that sound leaving her lips.

Fuck, who knew phone sex could be this amazing?

Blood races through my veins like wildfire, lighting up every nerve ending. The sound of her short, halting breaths through the phone is making me insane. If I weren't an hour away, I'd drive over to her place right now and pound her into the wall.

"Landon, I'm close," she says.

Hell yeah. My fist moves in short, efficient strokes, trying to get there with her.

Until a loud, unwelcome bang hits the door, and my heart almost stops. *What the fuck?*

"Wrap it up, Covey! I need to piss!" Asher calls through the door, totally killing the mood.

Fuck.

I tuck my still-erect dick back into my jeans and pinch the bridge of my nose, hissing out a shaky exhale. "Be out in a second!" I call.

"Oh no he's not!" Aubree calls out to Asher, even though he can't hear her. She's not on speakerphone. Her moans and gasps were for my ears only.

"Shit, I'm sorry about this." I rub one hand over my face.

A huge groan of frustration pours out of Aubree. "This is awful. Your teammates suck. I hate them."

"I do too." I chuckle. "But I'll make it up to you when I get back. I promise."

"I'm going to hold you to that," she says.

I grin, despite the massive case of blue balls I'm sure I'll have later. "Please do."

CHAPTER FIFTEEN

This or That

Aubree

"Cats or dogs?" I'm sitting at the kitchen table in Landon's newly furnished apartment, twirling lo mein noodles around a set of chopsticks, and waiting for his answer to this obviously crucial, but very easy-to-answer question.

Our low-key evening started with a half-hour debate about what takeout to order and has turned into a full-on game of trying to agree on anything whatsoever. So far, Chinese food has been the only common ground we've found.

When Landon takes too long to answer, too preoccupied with his sweet-and-sour chicken, I repeat the question. "Cats or dogs? Come on, this is an easy one."

"Dogs," he says with a firm nod. "I like cats, but

they're kind of boring. I could see myself adopting a golden retriever someday. Maybe even two."

I wrinkle my nose. "Two big dogs is way too much. Two cats, on the other hand, is totally doable. They're so low maintenance."

"Because they're not any fun," he says, pointing a chopstick at me before grappling with a piece of chicken. After a few hilarious seconds of fumbling, he tosses the chopsticks aside and grabs a fork. It's oddly adorable. "I've got one. Chunky or smooth peanut butter? On three. One, two . . ."

At the same time, he says *chunky* and I say *smooth*.

Figures.

"I told you. We're opposites on everything." I reach across the table toward his plate of yummy-looking chicken, but he drags it away from my chopsticks.

"Why didn't you just order your own?"

Unamused, I frown at him, and he gives in, sectioning off a portion of chicken and scooting it onto my plate.

"Chinese food is meant for sharing, especially with your wife," I say with an eye roll. "I've never met anyone who just orders one thing and keeps it all to himself."

"Well, now you have. There's a first time for everything, right?" A smug grin tugs at his lips.

All bickering aside, there's a certain *first time* I'm sure we can both agree has been on our minds. The thought of our first time has been burning a hole in the back of my mind, well, for weeks now, but especially since he opened the door tonight looking so deliciously masculine.

The scruff on his jawline is a little grown out from his weekend away with the guys, and his bright blue eyes twinkle with excitement to see me. Whether we make it to the bedroom this evening or not, I'll be riding the high from that look in his eyes all night. There can't be any drug quite like knowing the man who has been occupying all your thoughts has missed the shit out of you too. Even if he is a stupid dog person.

"Okay, one more." Landon leans forward, determination flickering in his blue eyes. "I think we might actually agree on this one. Coffee or tea?"

I nod. "On my count. One, two . . ."

We're interrupted by the sound of my phone buzzing in my purse again and again.

"Sorry." I grab my bag off the back of my chair, digging through to silence the buzzing. But one look at my screen, and I know these aren't texts I can ignore.

"Holy shit!" I half gasp, half squeal.

Landon lifts a brow. "Everything okay?"

"Better than okay." I flip my phone around to show him the text from Elise, a picture of her left hand rocking a beautiful princess-cut diamond with a pair of twinkling sapphire side stones.

He whistles through his teeth. "Well, I'll be damned. Justin locked it down." Once the shock passes, his face breaks into a big cheesy grin. "Good for them. What an awesome couple."

"An awesome couple who will no doubt throw an awesome wedding."

Landon nods, popping another piece of sweet-and-sour chicken into his mouth. "And maybe we won't have to fly halfway across the country for this one."

I swat his arm with the back of my hand. "It's their day. They can get married wherever they want."

"Sure, but who wouldn't want to get married

here?" He gestures toward his floor-to-ceiling windows and the sunset-soaked skyline outside. This apartment really has the perfect view.

I push out of my chair, wandering toward the windows with Landon only a few paces behind me. The sun has nearly slipped beneath the horizon, casting a warm pink and orange glow across the park below.

"It really is a beautiful city," I whisper, soaking it all in. It's not often that I get to see Seattle from this high up.

Landon wraps his arms around my waist from behind, pulling me close enough to rest his chin on top of my head. "Just wait till the fall when all the leaves are changing colors."

And just like that, one little mention of the future turns my stomach into a ball of lead. He doesn't know it yet, but I won't even be in this country come fall. He'll be enjoying that view alone.

"I actually prefer summer," I lie, desperate to change the subject. I pull his arms a little tighter around my waist, like a seat belt holding me back from crashing into the truth.

Landon welcomes the closeness, squeezing me tight. "Good thing we still have two months left then."

My throat closes up, my lungs shriveling like old helium balloons. *Holy shit. He knows.* I stand there, frozen in his arms, too shocked to say a word.

Did my boss tell him? Or maybe he saw one of my emails from a potential landlord pop up on my phone. *Shit*, it doesn't matter *how* he found out, only that he *did* find out. From someone other than me.

I break out of his grip, swiveling toward him, but I can't even bring myself to look him in the eye. "I'm sorry I didn't tell you sooner."

It's quiet for a moment, and then, to my surprise, Landon laughs. "What, that summer is only three months long? Last I checked, you don't control the calendar."

Confused, I look up at him, trying to make sense of his crinkled features. "What are you talking about?"

"It's June, which means we have two months left of summer. Maybe three, if we're lucky and the weather cooperates. What are *you* talking about?"

I wish I could stop the flush creeping across my cheeks, but it's too late. Even my ears are already redder than the sunset. Of course he was referring to summer ending. Why the hell would he be talking about anything else?

"Are you okay?" he asks, leading me over to take a seat on the couch.

I must look like I'm about to pass out or something, because he disappears to the kitchen and returns with a glass of water, which I sip slowly.

"What's going on, Bree? You seem off. What did you think I already knew?"

My chest tightens as I stare down into the water glass, avoiding his gaze. This is it, Bree. You have to tell him. All I have to do is say four little words. "I'm moving to Vancouver." Easy peasy.

But when I open my mouth, the words get lodged in my throat, blocking my air until I swallow them back down. Because telling him comes with a whole host of questions I don't know the answers to.

What will happen to us? Would we even work long distance? It would certainly come with challenges, and we haven't been together long enough for me to ask him to sacrifice like that. Are we even considered a couple other than on paper?

"I'm . . . just tired," I finally manage to say. "I haven't slept much the past few days. I should get going."

He nods, dragging his thumb along my cheek before pressing a gentle kiss against my lips. "Stay the night."

My breath halts in my chest. "What?"

"Stay the night with me," he says again, tucking a loose strand of hair back into my messy bun, letting his fingers linger for a moment at the nape of my neck. "I've got an extra toothbrush, and I cleared out a drawer for you in my dresser."

"I can't."

His forehead creases. "Why not?"

"I just can't, Landon," I mutter as I get up off the couch and lunge for my jacket. "I have to go home." My stomach churns with guilt, but I need space. And fresh air. And to get out of here before I say something I'll regret.

"Is it something I said?"

The hurt in his voice stops me in my tracks. I can't stay, but I can't leave him hurt and confused like this. I sigh, pivoting on my heel, and lock eyes with the most deflated, disappointed man I've ever seen. Just one look at him is enough to break a girl's heart.

"You didn't do anything wrong," I say. "I'm just . . . not ready." It's not much of an excuse, but it's easier than the truth—that there's no use playing house with him when my time here has an expiration date.

"If you won't stay over, will you at least take your SUV? I can't stand to stare at it another day."

"Fine." I hold one hand out, palm up. "Where are the keys?"

Pushing to his feet, he heads for the console table and digs the key fob out of the drawer. With a sad smile, he presses it into my palm, then curls my fingers around it, holding my closed fist in his hand.

"Drive safe, okay? Make sure to adjust the seat and mirrors."

"I will," I say on a shaky breath.

If only he knew that pretty soon, this city will be in my rearview mirror. And so will he.

CHAPTER SIXTEEN

First Timer

Landon

Our plane touched down in Dallas thirty minutes ago, and we've only just gotten our checked luggage when I get a text from the groom's mother.

> Can you pick up the vases from the florist?

And then an address follows.

> Sure thing, I reply.

I told Owen to pass my number along to his parents in case they needed help with anything. I guess he took that to heart.

"Looks like we're going to run a little errand to

the florist. That okay with you?" I ask Aubree.

"I'm game, as long as we get to eat lunch after."

"Deal. I'm starved too."

The Dallas heat is oppressive. It seems to suck all the air from my lungs the moment we exit the airport terminal to head to the parking garage to get our rental car.

I know the rest of the guys were hooked up with sweet rides from luxury dealerships—Porsches and Ferraris and who knows what else. My silver sedan is modest, and while there's not a thing wrong with it, I can't help but feel a little sheepish. My salary doesn't command the buying power theirs does, plain and simple. Maybe someday, but today is not that day.

Aubree doesn't seem to mind at all, tossing her bag in the trunk next to mine and hopping into the passenger seat. She cranks the air-conditioning to full blast as soon as I push the ignition.

"Holy hell. People live here?" She groans, lifting her long hair off the back of her neck and fanning herself with one hand.

Stifling is too tame a word. It's hard to breathe. Hard to think. But as soon as that cold air fills the car, we both relax a little. I get us to the interstate and navigate to the address on my phone.

After that chore is done, we're on our way to the Four Seasons Hotel, where we'll be staying and where the wedding will be tomorrow. I never even realized Becca was from Dallas.

The lobby is massive with tall ceilings and gold chandeliers. It's opulent and classic, and a little over the top. Basically, it's perfect for a wedding.

As we get checked in, we learn we're not staying in the hotel itself. A suited attendant in a golf cart arrives to drive us down a winding path along the golf course to where private villas dot the landscape. Once our bags are inside our villa and I've tipped the guy, we're alone for the first time today.

Aubree turns toward me and smiles shyly. "Hey."

I have no idea what she's thinking. "Hey."

"There's only one bed." She nods toward the massive bed dominating the center of the villa's bedroom.

"Don't get any ideas now."

She lifts one brow. "You're not worried I'm going to take advantage of you, are you?"

"Worried? No. Hopeful? Yes." She laughs, her eyes dancing on mine.

It's nice to see her smiling again. The last time we hung out at my apartment, things felt kind of strained. Aubree made some excuse about being tired and rushed out. But at least she took the SUV I got her, so maybe I'm reading too much into it. Maybe she was just tired.

"You want to get changed, and then we'll wander around this place and find Owen's mom? Get some lunch too?"

She nods, "If we're changing, I'm going to put my swimsuit on."

"Good plan." It's hotter than Satan's asshole out there and a dip in the pool sounds amazing.

The resort is immaculately maintained from the neat stone walkways to the manicured shrubs. Aubree takes in everything, walking along beside me wearing a pair of oversize black sunglasses.

When her hand slips into mine, there's a sudden rush of relief, followed by a sharp pinch in my chest. I haven't held hands with a woman in years. Honestly, I can't remember the last time. There have been make-out sessions in the back of dark clubs, and even a hand job in the back of a taxi once, but nothing was as life-changing as the feel of her hand in mine.

Shooting me a shy smile, Aubree keeps right on walking beside me like she didn't just rock my entire world.

I feel my phone buzz in my pocket and pull it out. "Owen's mom just finished a meeting with the caterer," I say, pocketing my phone. "Her text asked if I could meet her in the lobby."

"Sure." Aubree nods.

My first thought when I finally meet Owen's mom face-to-face? A drunken conversation that took place during a trip to Boston last year.

"My mom has a dildo," Owen said somberly, his face twisted.

The room went deadly silent. Until we all burst into laughter.

Unfazed, Owen went on. "It has, like, a hook on the end." He made a curving motion with his finger.

"Oh my God, please stop." Justin groaned.

"Why the fuck do you know this?" I asked.

"Because, when you're a kid, you're always

rummaging around in drawers," he said, like that somehow explained everything.

I shudder at the memory. And now I have to look into her eyes and try to pretend I don't know what her dildo looks like. *Good times. Fucking kill me now.*

"Hello, Mrs. Parrish," I say to the stocky silver-haired woman standing in front of me.

"Landon Covington. Look at you. Wow. Even taller in person than I imagined you'd be." Her eyes dance on mine, moving between me and Aubree like she's amused by something. I have no idea what Owen could have told her, but based on the fact he has zero filter, I'm guessing it was a lot.

I force my lips into a grin, nodding at her. "This is my date, Aubree. We picked up those vases. They're boxed up in the back of my rental car."

"Perfect. Thank you for doing that. And it's nice to meet you, Aubree." She nods. "Just bring them to the ballroom in the morning by ten, please," she says, meeting my eyes again. "It's down that hallway." She points to the far end of the grand lobby, where a wide marble hall branches off.

"Can do."

After that, we're free to grab lunch, which we do by the pool. This place is lush and private and gorgeous. Seeing this, I think I've figured out how people survive Texas summers—they stay in the water.

And that's exactly what Aubree and I do for the rest of the afternoon. Eating club sandwiches and fries in lounge chairs, rubbing sunblock onto each other's backs, splashing and laughing in the crystal-blue water of the pool. And definitely not worrying about what will happen later.

Okay, that last part is a lie. I'm totally preoccupied with what might happen tonight in our villa. It will be the first time Aubree and I have spent together in a bed since Vegas.

I have no idea if tonight could be the night, and I don't want to put any pressure on her, but I'm down with whatever might happen.

Later, after we've each had a shower and dressed, we share a quick kiss before we head off in different directions—her to the bride's dinner, and me to the groom's dinner.

"Dang, dude, this place is bomb," Jordie says, taking in the immaculate private dining room where the dinner for Owen is being held.

Most of the team is here, along with Owen's family—his male cousins, uncles, dad, and grandpa. A buffet of barbecue has been laid out, and lawn games are set up just beyond French doors leading to lush grass outside. It's all pretty chill.

I'm fixing myself a plate of smoked brisket when our team's captain, Grant, comes over to me, a beer bottle dangling from his hand.

"Hey. Can I talk to you?" he asks with a somber look.

Shit. A sinking feeling settles low in my stomach. I have no idea what's put the stern expression on his face, but I only hope it's not bad news about my spot on the team roster. I may not have been here long, but I feel like I've finally found my place, like I belong here.

"Yeah, sure." I take my plate and follow him to the far end of the room that's currently empty. I take a seat and set down my plate, then cross one ankle over my knee.

Grant sits next to me, and his gaze moves to my foot. "Dude, where are your socks?"

My tailored suit pants have risen up, revealing a few inches of skin. When I got dressed, I shoved my bare feet into leather loafers, thinking no one would notice.

Shrugging, I say, "You don't need socks when you're awesome."

He merely shakes his head. "Kids these days."

I'm aware that Grant is thirty-two, one of nine guys on the team who are over the age of thirty. Sports commentators like to make a big deal about things like this, noting the experience of our lines and who might be likely to retire. As far as I can tell, Grant is in his prime and won't be hanging up his skates anytime soon. Which is a damn good thing as far as the Ice Hawks franchise is concerned, because he's a steady and reliable leader, a good teammate, and a great captain. And let's not forget one of the best players in the league. Only, I have no idea what he wants with me, or why he's called me over to this private corner.

Faking nonchalance, I force myself to fork up a bite of my dinner and bring it to my mouth. "So, what's up, man?" I ask around a mouthful of tender brisket.

Grant exhales a long sigh. "Wanted to talk to you about something."

My stomach turns over again, but I force myself to swallow the bite of food. "Sure. Anything."

He nods and meets my eyes. "I know the guys have been giving you a hard time about this whole quickie wedding thing."

"Uh, yeah." I take another bite of food without tasting it.

"Well, I wanted to cut the shit and find out, all joking aside, how you're really doing."

Wait. What? Grant—grumpy-ass, growly Grant—wants to know about my emotional state? This is an unexpected development.

I'm about to make a joke, to laugh and assure him I'm fine, but something in his eyes gives me pause. He's being real with me, and I owe him the same.

I take a deep breath and push my plate away. "Honestly?"

He nods. "Of course."

"Things are pretty fucking confusing."

His expression is measured, serious. And suddenly I find myself wondering if Grant's ever been in love.

"Go on," he says, nodding his encouragement at me.

"Well, the thing was a joke, right? A drunken Vegas shenanigan. Except, for me, I'm not sure that's all it is."

"Why's that?" he asks, and my mind spins.

Because it's never been like this for me before. I like her as a person. As a partner. As a woman. It's crazy how well we get along, even if there's a lot of shit we don't agree on. Being near her is just effortless. Take this trip, for instance. Isn't travel supposed to be stressful? Not with Aubree. We may not agree on everything, but cats versus dogs aside, we just click. We have from that very first night in Vegas. But I can't tell him all that.

Finally, I say, "Because I take marriage seriously. Because I like her. Because . . . I don't know. Maybe it's stupid, or immature, or whatever. But I really like her. Shouldn't that mean something?"

Grant's mouth presses into a line as though he's considering the weight of my words. "Okay. That's what I thought. I've only known you a short time, but I've never seen you blow off your commitments or not give something your best. Everything you do, you give it your all, and I respect that."

I nod, struck silent by the things he's noticed about me. "What's your take on all this?" I really don't want to hear him caution me away from Aubree, or tell me I'm being foolish or to be careful. But he's my captain and he's pulled me aside, so it seems only right to get his take on things.

Grant's expression is stern as he meets my eyes. "It's possible there could be blow-back on the team. Aubree's role—the organization she works for is affiliated with the team, and our rookie has just gotten hitched . . ." He pauses, taking a breath. "But I don't think that'll happen. And if it was going to get out, it would have by now."

I feel pretty foolish that it never occurred to me. "Right," I say with a nod.

"But as your captain and teammate, you've got my support." He nods once. "There's one other thing."

"What's that?"

"Don't let the guys give you a hard time. Trust yourself and follow your gut. It'll serve you well. You got me, rookie?"

An easy smile overtakes my face. "Yes, sir."

The rest of the evening passes without much excitement. There's food and cake, and some speeches by Owen's older male relatives.

I end up spending more time with them than I'd planned, and by the time I make it back to the villa, Aubree is asleep, curled on her side, facing away from me. I hoped for some alone time with her tonight. And before your mind jumps into the gutter—no, I don't mean like that (although I wouldn't have minded, for the record.) It's just that I barely saw her today, outside of our couple of hours by the pool.

Disappointed, I change out of my suit and slip into bed beside her, careful not to wake her.

There's always tomorrow, I guess.

• • •

I spend the next afternoon running a few more last-minute errands for the bridal party. This time, my talents have been loaned out to Becca's mom—those talents being that I have a car and know how to use my GPS. Apparently, the florist forgot to include a corsage for Becca's grandmother, so I went to pick up the hastily made replacement, and a few more stops besides.

I make it back just in time for the wedding ceremony to begin.

The guests are all seated under a huge white

tent in rows of little gold-adorned chairs, and a harpist strums a soft melody that makes the whole thing feel enchanted. From the sidelines, the wedding coordinator gets us lined up in the correct order, and then I'm taking Aubree's hand to escort her down the aisle. When I left this morning, she was still dressed in the hotel robe with her hair wet from the shower. Now she's . . . breathtaking.

Her pale pink dress brushes the ground and hugs her body in all the right places. I have to curl my hands into fists just to keep them to myself. I want to run my fingertips along her spine, feel the warmth of her skin, and know if she'll shiver under my touch.

"Made it back just in time," she whispers as we make our way down the aisle to the front of the gathering.

"You look incredible," I whisper back.

Aubree's lips twitch, but she keeps her eyes straight ahead.

Once the wedding party is all in place, the music changes to something more classic. Becca, in a formfitting white lace gown, begins making her way down the aisle toward where Owen is standing stock-still, gazing at her with an awe-filled expression.

When she reaches her destination, they share a smile and a couple of hushed whispers before Becca straightens his bow tie with a smirk.

The officiant smiles warmly at the crowd. "Friends and family of Owen Parrish and Becca Phillips, you have all been invited here today to witness and celebrate the deep, uniting love these two share."

One of Becca's friends from college reads a poem I'm not familiar with. Something about finding the strength to let yourself be vulnerable. It's not very wedding themed, but it fits somehow with Owen and Becca. For as long as I've known them, which admittedly isn't all that long, I've seen how fiercely they love each other. And to do that, I guess you have to be vulnerable.

The officiant recites a scripture next about a woman leaving her family to join with a man, and then the rings are brought up by Owen's dad.

When it's Owen's turn to read his vows, a huge lopsided grin overtakes his face. He launches in with barely a breath, like he's been waiting to say these words to her forever.

"Your strength is humbling. Your confidence is

addicting. And your beauty inside and out is beyond anything I could have hoped for, or deserved
in a partner." He clears his throat. "I promise to be
yours, faithfully, until my final breath. I love you
now and forever, Becca."

When it's Becca's turn, she has to take a moment to compose herself and wipe her eyes, because Owen's heartfelt words have made her cry. I
look around and see there's hardly a dry eye in the
entire place.

Then she takes a shaky breath and lifts her
chin. And when she meets Owen's eyes, something
inside me twists. She's gazing at him with so much
emotion in her eyes, I feel a little breathless.

I want that. I want someone to look at me the
way Becca is looking at Owen—like he's her whole
world, and she'd be lost if he wasn't in it.

I hardly hear the words coming out of her
mouth, but their effect on Owen is immediate. My
always-down-for-a-good-time buddy, the competitive hockey player I've come to know this past
year, is gone. In his place is a six-foot-four wall of
trembling emotion. He sniffs, his eyes watering as
her words move him to tears.

"I'll always be by your side, through every

high and every low," she says in a small, but sure voice. "When I realized the truth, that I loved you in a way that was big and messy and not something that could be contained, I was scared." She swallows and pauses, her lip trembling. "Terrified, actually. But then you made it all better, just like you've done with every worry, every heartache I've experienced, every fear I had. I love you too, Owen." She wipes away a tear tumbling down his cheek and smiles warmly at him.

The officiant announces them as husband and wife, and Owen lunges forward, lifting Becca into his arms. She squeals with surprise, then touches his jaw, guiding his mouth to hers in a sweet, slow kiss.

The guys on the team cheer loudly, and everyone claps.

Then there are photos and a champagne toast, and afterward, we're all herded into a huge ballroom for the reception.

All throughout dinner, I'm distracted. Agitated. Aubree, on the other hand, seems calm and collected—dancing on the parquet dance floor with the girls, participating in the bouquet toss with the bridesmaids, and eating my slice of cake when I tell her I'm not interested. My knee bounces with nervous energy beneath the white linen tablecloth, and I hope she can't tell how fucking fidgety I am.

"Should we dance?" she asks.

"Sure." I stand and offer her my hand, trying to act like everything is normal.

Aubree slides her palm into mine, and I guide us to the center of the dance floor. The happy bride and groom are moving to the music. Most of the wedding party is on the dance floor too. Becca's bridesmaids, being led by Owen's sister Elise, are making up some kind of coordinated dance involving several complicated steps. I think the champagne has officially kicked in.

Grinning up at me, Aubree brings her hands to my shoulders as we begin to move.

"Having a good time?" I ask.

She nods. "It's so beautiful."

She's right. The wedding has been romantic and heartfelt. It also couldn't have been any further from mine and Aubree's drunken, giggle-filled ceremony. Becca and Owen had cried as they recited the vows they'd written themselves. Honestly, it was pretty cool to witness. Aubree deserves a wedding like this, but instead she got a quickie Vegas wedding.

The music changes to a slow waltz. I don't know how to waltz, but I love just having her in my arms.

As we dance together, my gaze drifts down to hers, and I'm overcome with emotion. Despite the fact I'm planning to strip her naked (and soon, I hope), my eyes lock onto hers, communicating a promise—that I'll always be careful with her. That I want her in a way I've never wanted anyone before.

• • •

Hours later, after what is arguably the best wedding reception I've ever been to, we make it back to our villa. But I'm feeling no more settled than I was at dinner. The villa is dark except for a bedside lamp that glows softly across the room.

Pausing once we're inside, I turn her body toward mine. "I'm not sure if I told you before, but you look incredible."

Aubree smiles. "You might have mentioned something."

She touches my chest, using me for balance as she steps out of her high heels one by one. I steady her with one hand on her waist, my mouth twitching at how our height difference becomes even more exaggerated once she's barefoot.

My heart thuds restlessly inside my chest. I ache for her, but I have no idea what she's thinking. But then she lifts on her toes, bringing her mouth to mine, and I get my first indication about how she wants tonight to go.

"Bree." I breathe out her name on an exhale when her hands slip down the front of my chest, under my tuxedo jacket, and settle at my belt buckle.

"Tell me if—"

"*Yes,*" I blurt out gracelessly. *Yes to everything.*

Aubree hums out a chuckle as I get to work unzipping her dress. Is it weird that I studied where the zipper was located while she danced with Sara? Left side, the clasp just below her elbow.

Once it's unzipped, the dress falls to her feet, and Aubree steps out of it. She's so stunning in her nude bra and matching lace panties that I go momentarily still.

It goes without saying that I don't know what I'm doing. Everything between us is new, and so it's pure instinct when I lift her into my arms. Aubree drapes her arms around my shoulders and wraps her legs behind my back. I hoist her higher, and when she feels the heavy weight of my arousal pressing between us, she makes a breathless sound and rocks against me, trying to get closer.

Hell.

My feet start moving and I carry her to the bed, depositing her ungracefully into the center. As I stand beside the bed, she attacks my belt buckle, working it free as I stare down at her in awe.

The heavy weight of this moment is filled with expectation, but I'm not nervous. Not even a little. She sets my skin on fire with a simple touch, and I want her more than I've ever wanted anything, including my spot on an NHL team.

But while I'm not nervous, I am desperate. The idea of her hands on me tonight has me all kinds of lit up. We've touched and kissed and done a dozen other sinful things, which means that so far, tonight shouldn't feel any different. But blood thunders through my veins because I know that tonight will change *everything*.

I tilt her chin up and lean down to capture her mouth in a sweet, slow kiss. At least, I intend it to be slow, but when she parts her lips and touches her tongue eagerly to mine, I lose control.

I crawl across the bed, Aubree scooting to accommodate me until we're lying side by side, kissing. My hands roam over her curves, touching the soft dip in her stomach, lingering over her breasts.

A deep groan pours out of me the second her hand slips beneath my boxers. Aubree smiles at my response.

Biting her lip, she watches me as her hand moves slowly up and down my entire length as she draws me out of my black boxers. "I don't think I'll ever get used to this."

Her cheeks are flushed and rosy. I love the idea that maybe my body excites her as much as hers does me.

"I really love your dick," she says next, still biting that lip as she gazes at my length, almost like she's sizing me up.

My entire body clenches with need. "It's all yours," I choke out on a halting breath.

"Are you sure about this?" Her expression turns serious, and her hand stops against me.

"Fuck yeah, I'm sure."

"I mean about *me*. You've waited . . . Are you sure I'm the person you want to do this with?"

"Aubree, you're it. You're what I want. No one but you."

She's breathing hard when she meets my eyes. "Because we don't have to."

"Please." The word tumbles out of my mouth without my permission. "I need it. I want you more than I've ever wanted anyone before." I touch her cheek, and she gives me a nod.

Then Aubree leans over me, her long hair brushing my chest as she kisses the hollow of my throat, my chest, down my abs.

"This might need to be a quickie," I warn, slightly breathless, touching her hair.

She ignores me, continuing to kiss a path down my stomach until she reaches the trail of hair below my belly button. Then she moves even lower, and my abs tighten as she licks along my rigid shaft and makes a little happy sound.

Fuck.

I watch as she wraps me in her fist, stroking as she closes her mouth over me. With the perfect amount of pressure, she sucks me urgently into the depths of her warm mouth. It feels fantastic.

And when she bobs lower, applying firm suction, my toes curl and a deep groan rumbles inside my throat. It's so good, but I should stop her. This isn't how I want tonight to go. But I'm powerless. Aubree's sucking on me like I'm the best thing she's ever tasted.

I curse out a warning. "Baby, fuck . . . *fuck*."

She doesn't heed my warning until I'm pulsing hotly into her mouth, spilling on my abs. There's so much, but Aubree doesn't stop her perfect torture, stroking and licking the whole time. I'm dizzy. Breathless.

Holy hell. That was intense.

"Shit. I didn't mean to . . ." I grab some tissue from beside the bed and clean the mess off my abs.

"Shh." She quiets me with a soft kiss pressed to my jawline. "I wanted you to."

"But why?"

"So when we have sex, you can last longer."

"Oh." A hazy smile overtakes my lips. "My wife is absolutely brilliant."

She laughs. "Did that feel good?"

"It felt fucking incredible. You're amazing."

I pull her into my arms and roll us over so I'm on top of her. I kiss her neck, her mouth, her hair. My mouth covers hers in a dizzying kiss, which Aubree returns with much enthusiasm.

"Then this is going to feel even better," she says, bringing one hand between us.

I'm about to tell her I need a minute to recover, but then I realize, no, I actually don't. Somehow I'm already straining and ready to go again. Aubree parts her thighs, rubbing her center up and down over me enticingly.

"Condom?" I croak, my voice deep.

"We're married, Lovey. We don't need one, do we?"

For a moment, I'm speechless. I just figured we would use one. "I'm clean," I say.

"Me too. And I'm on the pill."

I recall the package of birth control pills I saw on the bathroom counter. "Whatever you want. It's your call. If you want me to wear one, I brought some."

She smirks and tosses her hair over one shoulder. "I love that you came prepared, but I'm not fucking my husband with a condom on."

I let out a shaky laugh because Aubree is full of surprises. She's also rubbing herself against me in the most amazingly distracting way. "I would love to feel you bare. Just didn't know that would be an option."

"I trust you," she murmurs, and my heart clenches.

And then Aubree finds the right angle, and I join us with a long, slow thrust.

Holy. Fucking. Shit.

Pausing once, I pull back, hesitate for a second, and then press deeper. Aubree makes a low needy sound as pleasure shoots down my spine.

"Oh fuck, Landon. You're so . . ."

I pause again, enjoying the feel of her body yielding to mine. "More?"

Her knees widen, accepting more of me. "Yes, more."

I pant out hot, heavy breaths with each slide of my body inside hers. Every emotion feels raw. Every moment is drenched in pleasure. It's almost too much. Groaning, I bury myself deep, gripping her hip in one hand until I'm fully buried in the tightest, hottest thing I've ever felt.

"Tell me how it feels," she murmurs.

But I can't.

I can't speak.

Can't breathe.

The only thing I can do is feel. And, *holy shit*, does it feel amazing. It's hot and wet and perfect.

The potent sense of satisfaction is so primal, it renders me speechless. I've been waiting all my life for a feeling like this to hit me. And now it has, and I'm so far out of my element, it's not even funny. Falling for Aubree is like playing goalie without pads, and the hits just keep on coming.

Lust shoots through me, skewering my heart, and I'm gone. I've fallen for this girl.

"Landon," she murmurs.

"It's so good," I say on a groan. "Fuck, you're incredible . . ."

"More," she says softly. "Yes, there."

She pants hot against my throat when I shift my

hips up, finding an angle that makes her shiver in my arms.

"Oh, Landon," she whimpers, shaking with need. "Don't stop. Just. Like. That."

There's no way in hell I'm stopping, but the amount of restraint it takes to maintain *Just. Like. That.* is no small achievement. Especially when all I want to do is slam into her like some kind of wild animal in heat. Thankfully, I resist that urge, but just barely. I want to make this good for her too.

Because so far? This is the best night of my entire life.

• • •

Aubree

A gasp of satisfied hunger pushes past his parted lips. "You're mine now, Bree," Landon growls into the heat of my throat.

The pleasure is so blinding, I squeeze my eyes closed and hiss out an uneven breath. How is this moment even real?

I've never been this overwhelmed, this overcome by desire before. It's like I'm hyperaware of every little thing. From Landon's sweet, drugging kisses to the way my body stretches to accommodate him, to the exquisite little growling sounds he's making as he sinks deeper inside me.

He started slow, tentative at first, almost like he was testing me, testing his weight above me, testing how much of his thick length I could take. But now his hips rock urgently into mine, his powerful thrusts sending fractures of heat racing through every nerve ending.

This is supposed to be about him, not me. But as Landon moves above me, bliss spirals through every cell in my body, sweeping out everything else until I'm nothing more than a tangle of heat and lust, threatening to burst into flames, consumed by a wildfire of sensations that burn hotly through me.

His eyes are focused, unblinking, and the muscles in his jaw flex. "You feel incredible," he groans, his wide chest rumbling with the sound.

This situation between us might be uncertain, and all kinds of crazy, but something about this man makes all common sense fly out the window, while simultaneously cranking my libido up to an eleven. I want him in a way I've never wanted anyone before.

With my emotions in a tangled knot, I draw a

shaky inhale. I tried not to fall for this man—my husband—but I know in this moment my attempts were futile. Looking into Landon's eyes, watching him sink deep inside me for the first time, feeling his possessive caresses all over my skin . . . I realize that guarding my heart was pointless.

"You do too," I say on an exhale. It's the truth. His body is a finely honed machine of muscle and power, and *damn*, does he know how to use it. In fact, there's one muscle in particular that's exceeded all my expectations.

His breath rasps unevenly against my throat, hot and loud and urgent. His hips roll forward, pressing deep, deep enough to unlock something new inside me, and a jolt of pleasure makes me gasp. *Holy shit.*

"There?" he asks, breathing hard.

Trembling, I moan, so close already.

"Yeah, baby?" He thrusts deep again, and I pant out his name.

He takes direction well, studying what I like, lingering in the spots that make me moan and quake, quickly becoming the best lover I've ever had. *Holy unexpected plot twist.*

He claims my mouth again, his tongue touching mine in soft strokes like we have all the time in the world. And maybe we do.

I've thought about what our first time might be like. Of course I did. But it was nothing like *this*. No, *this* is way better than I ever imagined.

Stroking his tongue with mine, I wrap my legs around his waist, bringing his impressive length in even more. Landon stiffens, his mouth halting on mine.

"Aubree, *fuck*."

With my legs still wrapped around him, I trail my hands along his broad shoulders, absolutely enthralled with the feel of his big, muscular body moving over mine.

The sensation inside me builds, and I can't hold it back any longer. It crashes over me in a sweeping wave, and I fly apart, breathing hard and clutching his rock-hard ass as my body constricts tighter. The feeling peaks, drenching me in heat.

He makes a low pleasure-filled sound, his eyes opening to find mine as he feels me coming for him. "That. Feels—" He groans. "So. Fucking. Good." His wide chest trembles as though he can barely contain himself.

I press my lips to his neck, tasting his skin, loving the scratchy feel of his stubble along my cheek. We're both breathing hard, and I push my hands into his hair, turning his face to mine so I can kiss him again.

"I'm going to . . ." He groans. "Should I . . ."

I shake my head. "Inside me."

With shaky breaths, Landon's measured thrusts become erratic, uneven, and he curses again, pressing his face against my neck. Then I feel it . . . his warmth inside me as he makes one last low noise of pleasure.

Holy hell, that was intense.

Long before I'm ready for him to, he moves carefully off me, withdrawing slowly as he breaks our connection. I miss the heat of him immediately.

"That was . . ." Breathless, he pauses, his hair a rumpled mess from my roaming fingers. His dark eyebrows push together as he studies me. "Was it okay? For you, I mean? For me, it was fucking amazing."

I smile at him, trailing my fingers along his defined jaw. "It was amazing for me too."

Landon returns my smile, and my heart squeezes.

Never in a million years did I expect to be *here*. Yet, here we are, in this perfect moment, and I can't deny how right it feels.

I won't let myself think any scary thoughts about the future right now . . . I just enjoy the feel of his strong arms around me as he pulls me even closer. I nestle into the warmth of his firm chest and close my eyes, content for now to be exactly where I am.

CHAPTER SEVENTEEN

Coming Back for Seconds

Aubree

The morning sun filtering through the curtains stirs me awake.

Between dancing the night away at the reception and our private after-party back here at our villa, our beauty rest was well earned. Still, if given the option, I'd stay here in bed with Landon all day, alternating between sleep and sex. But we promised our friends we'd grab brunch with them this morning, so unfortunately that's not an option.

Rubbing the sleep from my eyes, I blink up at Landon, who has so graciously served as my pillow for the night. His lips are parted slightly, and soft snoring sounds vibrate through him.

With all the nervous excitement about his first time, I sort of forgot that this is also our first time sleeping together in the literal sense. Usually, I toss and turn throughout the night, battling stress dreams and waking up in a convoluted mess of wrapped-up sheets and ejected pillows. But last night, I didn't move from my spot tucked into the crook of Landon's arm, my cheek pressed against his firm chest.

Careful not to wake him, I peel myself out of his arms, then tiptoe to the bathroom as quietly as possible. When I return, I see that my attempt to be quiet was a bust. He's sitting upright in bed, his dark hair tousled from either sex or sleep or both, shooting me an adorable, sleepy smile.

"Good morning, gorgeous." His voice is raspier than usual first thing in the morning, rumbling low in his chest. It's sexy, to say the least.

"Good morning to you too. How'd you sleep?"

"Like a fucking rock."

He stretches his arms over his head, waking up his sleepy muscles. It makes me regret turning down his past invites to spend the night with him. Watching my shirtless husband stretch and flex his muscular arms in our shared bed is more than a little bit of a turn-on.

It's at this point that I realize that I'm standing

here, totally naked, having a completely normal conversation. Even if he is my husband, it feels a little odd to be this exposed to him in a totally non-sexual situation. I wander toward my suitcase to dig out a sleep shirt and slip it over my head. When I settle onto the edge of the bed, Landon looks at me like I just committed a crime.

"What'd you do that for?"

My brows scrunch together. "What are you talking about?"

His mouth crooks up as he shakes his head in disapproval. "Why the hell did you put on a shirt when you know I'm just going to take it right back off?"

My lips part, my breath catching in my throat. Before I can formulate a response, he's pulling me into his arms, peeling my shirt up and over my head before tossing it right back toward my suitcase.

"Much better." He growls against my neck, his hands gripping my hips while he trails kisses down the column of my throat. He cups my breasts firmly in his hands, giving one nipple the slightest flick with his thumb, then the other.

Instantly, any leftover sleepiness is pushed out of my system, replaced instead with pure, unadulterated need.

"Shit." I shudder against his touch as he slowly takes one nipple between his lips, teasing me. He's good at that. Electricity jolts through me, and I buck in pleasure.

He grins up at me, his blue eyes flickering mischievously as he slowly pulls back from my breasts, bringing his attention to lower. He touches between my thighs, testing my wetness. And based on the groan of approval I get, I take it he likes what he finds.

"I want to fuck you," he rasps out, his voice husky.

He may lack subtlety, but the rough edge to his voice makes my pulse jump. He wants me. And by the way the sheets are tented beneath him, he's ready for me too.

I press against his shoulders, easing him back onto the bed so I can climb on top of him. "Can we try it like this?"

"God, yes," he pleads on a shaky exhale.

I push the sheets aside, aligning myself with his full, impressive erection. Maybe it's just morning wood, but it's incredible that he's so hard for me already. I grip his base, giving his thick shaft a few precursory strokes. When I lean in to kiss him, he teases my clit with his thumb until I can't bear to wait another moment.

Another second of foreplay would be torture. I need him inside me. *Now*.

One slow, deliberate inch at a time, I lower myself onto him, and the second he's inside me, we moan in unison. How the hell does this feel even better than it did last night? I've only taken half of him when his hands clamor for my hips, easing me down until I've taken every last inch of his length.

"Holy f-fuck," I stutter, trying desperately to find my breath.

He squeezes my hip for reassurance. "That okay?"

Okay? It's more than okay. It feels more heavenly than I thought was possible on this earth.

But right now, I can't possibly form a sentence, so I meet the question with action, rocking my hips against him slowly, guiding him to the place deep inside me that I know will be my total undoing. He moans my name, my full name—Aubree, not Bree—over and over as I ride him, my hands pressed against his shoulders as he holds tight to my ass.

"I'm so close, baby," he says through clenched teeth, his thumb circling my clit as he rocks his hips against mine.

"Me too," I pant.

As soon as the words leave my lips, my body follows, twitching and pulsing until pleasure is pouring through me in slow, hot waves. I'm still riding my high as he falls over the edge after me, emptying himself into me in hot bursts. When he's totally drained, I collapse into him, resting my head against his heaving chest until my breath slows back to normal.

"Wow," he whispers, running his fingers through my hair. "How am I ever going to let you leave the bed now that I know how much fun that is?"

I smile against his chest. We lie there, intertwined with each other for a long, perfect moment before reality kicks back in. Unfortunately, it comes in the form of a weird noise coming from outside our door.

At first, I think it's knocking, and I frantically tug the sheets up to cover my naked self. But then the sound grows louder and louder, joined by a muffled holler worthy of the sidelines at an Ice Hawks game.

And that's when it hits me. It's not knocking outside our door. It's applause.

Am I in the middle of some twisted dream, or do we have a freaking audience?

I shoot up in bed, scrambling to grab my phone from the end table. It's 10:28. Almost a half hour *after* we agreed we'd meet our friends for brunch. So, yeah, that would be them outside our door.

"Oh my God," I blurt, showing him the time.

I can hardly make words happen right now, but Landon seems surprisingly unfazed. He just chuckles, raking his fingers through his messy hair before shoving back the sheets.

"Well, I guess we shouldn't leave our friends waiting."

I'm awestruck at how casual he is about this, but one look at the smirk on his lips has me smiling right along with him. I guess at the end of the day, it doesn't really matter. Our curtains are drawn, so it's not like anyone saw anything. And who cares what our friends heard? At least now we don't have to figure out how to tell them that Landon's V-card has officially been swiped.

We fumble out of bed, scrambling to put on whatever clean clothes are on the top of our suitcases. I use the bathroom and dress quickly in a black-and-white striped T-shirt dress, strictly because it means not having to put together an outfit. Paired with my favorite pair of strappy sandals, I can almost pass for someone who tried this morning. I clean up last night's makeup that I forgot to take off, then brush my teeth, combing out my sex hair with my fingers. Yesterday's half updo has left me with a few curls intact, and with a swipe of deodorant and a quick brush of my teeth, I don't look half bad.

Meanwhile, Landon somehow is making a pair of cargo shorts look good, an almost impossible feat. That hockey player butt possesses magical powers, I swear.

"Ready to go?" He reaches out a hand, and I lace my fingers tightly through his.

"Ready as I can be in under five minutes." I catch one last glimpse of myself in the mirror, tucking back a stray hair. "You sure I look okay?"

"Gorgeous as always," he says, sweeping his thumb over my lower lip giving me one last gentle, grateful kiss. "Thank you again for last night. And this morning. And for . . . everything, for trying with me."

"Trust me, Landon." I give his hand a squeeze. "You were well worth the wait."

I suck in a deep breath as Landon flips the latch on our door and tugs it open, revealing our cheering group of friends on the stone patio. Justin puts two fingers into his mouth and lets out a piercing whistle, while Bailey breaks into the Ice Hawks' fight song.

These fricking idiots.

I squint into the sunlight as I follow Landon's lead out onto the patio, stepping into the oppressive heat. The cheers continue as Landon locks the door behind us, and Sara holds out a hand to high-five me. It feels like we're being bombarded by the paparazzi, not our friends.

"Good morning, guys," Landon says, trying and failing to mask the fact that he's smiling with pride.

"I'd say you had a real good morning." Justin snickers, clapping his teammate on the back.

Landon just keeps walking, his shoulders

pushed proudly back as we strut, hand in hand, past our friends and down the sidewalk toward the hotel restaurant.

"Holy stamina, Lovey!" Elise calls after us.

"Hey now." Justin scolds her, then jumps right back in with the whooping and hollering.

Landon looks over his shoulder at our adoring fans, shaking his head. "Fuck off," he says with a laugh. But he doesn't stop smiling for even a second.

His world? Officially rocked.

CHAPTER EIGHTEEN
Now What?

Landon

It's been three weeks since Owen and Becca's wedding, and Aubree and I have spent almost every night together—either at her place or mine. We've shared meals and conversation, and had a lot of sex. Sometimes I initiate it, and sometimes it's her. But it's always really, really hot.

We've grown closer, talked about every topic from work to goals to childhood memories to favorite vacation spots, you name it. I like coming home to her at night, like eating dinner with her and talking about our days. I love having her in my bed. And as good as things have been between us, I can't help but feel like we're overdue for an actual chat about our future and where we stand.

Because the only thing we haven't talked

about?

Us.

And the worry about that has settled over me like a weighted blanket. I've fallen for her. I can't picture my future without her, or maybe I just don't want to.

Owen and Becca have just returned from their honeymoon in Greece, and he's been bombarding the guys on the team with text messages and photos from their trip. So, when my phone chimes in the other room, I expect it to be another dozen or so pics of idyllic little white buildings perched above turquoise water.

"We get it, dude. Greece was incredible. Blah, blah, blah," I mutter as I make my way into the kitchen to retrieve my cell phone from the counter.

But the notification isn't for a text from Owen. It's a voice mail from Coach Dodd.

Thirty minutes later, I'm lingering in the doorway to his office. He spots me and waves me inside.

"Thanks for coming over on short notice. I prefer to do these things in person. We're a family, ya know?" Coach says, eyeing me from over the rims of his wire-framed glasses once I enter his top-floor office.

"Sure, no problem." I still don't know why I'm here. His voice mail was cryptic.

"Sit down."

I lower myself into the black leather chair in front of his desk, and wipe my sweating palms on the front of my pants.

He lets out a deep exhale and removes his glasses, tucking them into the front pocket of his shirt. "So, I have news, kid."

I nod, taking a deep breath. Part of me knew this conversation was coming. Call it a gut instinct or something, but I knew my time with the Ice Hawks couldn't last, as much as I wanted it to. I have no idea if I'm being sent down to the affiliate team or what his news is, but the expression on his face and his somber tone say enough. It's not good news.

"As of this morning, we've placed you on waivers. The other teams in the league have twenty-four hours to either make a claim and pick you up, or you'll be moving down."

I open my mouth to respond, but realize I have

no fucking clue what to say. It means my days as a Seattle Ice Hawk are over, at least for now. My time playing with the team I love, in the city that's become my home, with the guys who have become my best friends, is done. It stings much more than I thought it would.

But Coach goes right on like he didn't just change my entire world. "It's just business. You've done well for yourself, and I know you have a future in the league. Try not to sweat it, okay?"

"I, um . . ." I clear my throat. "Thanks for the opportunity." It sounds like something you're supposed to say, and I add, "I've loved being a part of this organization." That part is true.

He holds up one hand. "I know. It's a lot to take in, and probably unexpected, but there's something else."

Apparently, when word to the league went out that my contract was up for grabs, he got a call right away. From a coach he's friends with, and somewhere he thinks I'd be very happy, but he doesn't want to say where just yet. He goes over the fine print on how this all works, but I barely hear a thing.

"Any thoughts?" he asks.

"I need to speak to my wife."

"Oh, so you *are* married. The rumors were true then?" His mouth lifts with an amused expression.

"You . . . heard?" I scratch my temple.

Coach Dodd nods. "Of course I heard. I just maintain a very strict *don't ask, don't tell* policy when it comes to my players' personal lives."

I nod. "Makes sense, I guess."

"But this marriage . . . I take it it's not the Vegas-quickie-ceremony joke I heard it made out to be?"

I shift, uncomfortably. "No, sir. It's the real deal."

"Is she pregnant?"

God, he's about as subtle as a bull in a china shop. "No." At least, not that I know of, but we have been having a *lot* of sex, and I wouldn't hate it if she was.

He nods. "Understood. Well, then speak with your wife, and we'll talk through all the details in the morning. It's all going to work out fine, okay, kid?"

"Thanks, Coach."

The only thing running through my brain on the drive home is Aubree.

Worst-case scenario is I'm not picked up by another team and have to move to Wisconsin to take a pay cut and play for our affiliate team. Best-case scenario? Well, there is no best case, because I'm going to have to move. That much is certain. And I have no idea if Aubree will quit her job and come with me, or if she'll finally just say *fuck it* to this whole experiment and walk away from our marriage for good.

When I pull into my building's parking garage, I can't make myself get out of the car and go inside. Instead, I pull out my phone and dial Aubree while a knot forms in my stomach.

She answers on the third ring. "Hey," she says casually. "What's up?"

"Can I, ah, talk to you?"

"Um . . ." She hesitates. "Now? Can it wait until tonight? I've got a couple of documents I need to finish up."

"What about lunch?" I ask, looking at the clock on my dash. "Have you eaten yet?"

She must sense the worry in my voice because

she concedes. "I haven't. Do you want to come by the office? We can grab something quick and talk then."

"Yeah. I'll be there in . . . thirty, depending on traffic. That work?"

"Sure. I'll see you then."

The drive to Aubree's office is fairly simple, and though I've never been here before, I do know the area well. I find parking behind the two-story concrete block building and then let myself inside. There's a reception desk, but no one working behind it, so I wander around until I find her office. Her name is etched into a silver placard outside the door.

Aubree Derrick.

I pause, staring at it for a second.

We had the discussion once about if she'd ever want to change her name, not because I would ever pressure her to do so, but because I was genuinely curious about her stance on it. She said that as a modern, independent woman, she couldn't really ever see herself taking a man's name. I told her that was fine with me, but as I stare at this little sign, I find myself wishing it read **AUBREE COVING-TON**. And maybe if it did, everything wouldn't have to fall apart.

"Oh! You're here," Aubree says, rising to her feet and coming around the side of the L-shaped desk that takes up most of her small office. "Traffic must have been clear," she says, lifting up on her toes to press a quick kiss to my lips.

"Yeah, it was nonexistent."

I take her left hand, giving it a squeeze, and run my fingers along her wedding ring.

"Are you okay?" She meets my eyes with a look of concern. "You sounded a little . . . stressed on the phone."

I nod. "Yeah, but something's come up."

She licks her lips. "Something good or something bad?"

I consider her question. "I don't know yet."

An older man dressed in khakis with hair graying at his temples steps out of a nearby office and into the hall. He must have overheard us talking and has come out to investigate.

"Oh, David," Aubree says, appearing a little flustered. "This is Landon." She gestures toward me. "And this is my boss, David Stone."

I extend my hand toward him as he approaches. "It's nice to meet you."

"Landon, was it?" he asks, returning my handshake.

"Yes. I'm Aubree's husband."

"Oh." David's eyes widen and he lets out an uneasy laugh.

Obviously, Aubree never told him about me. I wish I could say that didn't bother me, but it does. It really, really fucking does.

"Well, that's um . . ." He clears his throat as if stalling. "You guys must be getting excited for the big move then."

"The big move?" I ask, my gaze darting between Aubree and her boss.

"Yes, to Vancouver," he says casually.

Completely confused, I slowly repeat, "Vancouver."

David's brow furrows even more. "Aubree's accepted a promotion to open and run the first international office for us."

All the blood drains from my face, and my stomach sours. "She has."

I don't pose it as a question because the pained look on Aubree's features says it all. She's been pretending this entire time. Playing house with me while simultaneously planning to leave. And not just leave me, but leave the entire fucking country.

Her boss is still talking, saying something about what a great opportunity this is, but I can't hear anything over the blood thundering in my ears. And when I look up, all I can see is the painful truth reflected back at me in Aubree's eyes.

"Landon," she says, taking a step closer.

I hold up one hand. "You know what? I just realized I don't have time for lunch. I'll talk to you later, okay?"

Without waiting to hear her answer, I turn, my feet already carrying me toward the door while my heart sinks into my stomach.

"Wait! Landon, please," Aubree calls after me, but I don't stop.

Completely numb, I speed through every light on the drive home, reaching my place in under twenty minutes. I've only just gotten inside the front door when it opens again.

Aubree's here.

I guess I'm not the only one who knows his way around a gas pedal.

She approaches slowly, like she's struggling to get her legs to work. I know the feeling well, because I'm struggling to make my lungs work. A shaky inhale is the best I've got.

"Why are you here?"

"We need to talk. Please let me explain," she begs.

I lean one hip against the kitchen counter, watching her. She's visibly upset. Her hands are trembling at her sides, and her mouth is pressed into a firm line.

"Congratulations on the promotion," I say, my voice devoid of emotion.

She makes a small sound and shoves her hands in her hair. "Landon, please."

"David seems nice. And Vancouver is, well . . ." I pause, scratching my temple. "I really don't fucking care, to be honest."

A single tear rolls down her cheek. "I'm sorry."

"Why didn't you tell me?" My voice is pained, and I don't bother hiding it.

She swallows and wipes away the tear with her thumb. "Because I had no idea what we were or if we'd even work. Because I needed more time. Because I was scared. Because I thought if I—"

"How long have you known?"

She pauses for a second to compose herself. "I was offered the job right after we got back from Vegas."

"That's perfect. You never took this marriage seriously, never took *me* seriously. You never gave me a shot like you said you would."

"I did, Landon. I was."

"But it doesn't matter now."

She takes a step closer, and I force my gaze away. I can't look at her right now.

Her words come out in a whisper. "What can I say? What can I do?"

"Tell me the truth," I say, my eyes narrowing on hers.

She licks her lips, thinking. "I thought if I never gave you my heart, I could never get hurt. Is that what you wanted to hear?"

"That's just perfect." Sarcasm drips from my

tone.

"Are you mad?" she whispers, taking another hesitant step toward me.

"Oh, I'm fantastic." The words are a bitter lie I force from my throat. I'm broken. Destroyed. I gave this marriage everything I had, and it still wasn't enough. "It's better that I know all this now."

"Landon," she says, but I hold up one hand.

"Just go. I don't want you here," I say, my voice raspy but firm. I don't look up, but a few seconds later, I hear her footsteps retreat and then the sound of the front door clicking shut.

Then I grab my phone from the counter and hurl it at the far wall, where it shatters with a loud, satisfying crack.

CHAPTER NINETEEN

Kicked in the Balls

Landon

The following morning, I blink against the sunlight and grab my phone from the bedside table where it's ringing. I fumble to answer it, ignoring the shattered screen.

"Hello?"

Coach Dodd's voice booms through the speaker. "I've got some good news for you, kid."

"Yeah?" I say, rubbing one hand over my face. I was kind of hoping yesterday had just been a dream. Sadly, it wasn't, and now I have to deal with the consequences of whatever's about to come next.

"How does Vancouver sound to you?"

Is this some kind of joke? "Excuse me?"

"They came through for you, kid. The coach is a friend of mine, and he knows how hard you've worked to get where you are. He's not just taking you as a favor to me or anything like that, I want you to know that. You've earned a spot there."

But Vancouver? I think. What are the chances?

They're an expansion team that opened up two years ago. I don't know much about their coaching staff, but the Vancouver Rebels are highly regarded. They're good. Good enough to make it to the playoffs last year.

Dodd goes on about how they're a solid team, that they play well together and have some of the more experienced players in the league. Which is why they're looking to round out their lines with some younger, up-and-coming talent—a.k.a. me.

"Wow. I'm . . . I don't know what to say."

"Well, you have time to figure that out. I'm sure the press will want some kind of statement, but in the meantime, I'm sending you an email with the details and copying your new coach, Bill Montgomery. Monty is an old college drinking buddy of mine. He's all bark, no bite. Don't worry, kid."

"Thanks for everything, Coach."

"You bet."

We end the call, and I force myself out of bed and into the shower. By the time I'm toweling off, my phone is ringing again.

It's Owen.

"Shit, man. Canada? Really?"

This is all so confusing. But then I glance at the TV and realize he has to be talking about my move and not Aubree's, since there's a scrolling bar on the sports channel announcing moves, and my name is one of them. Plus, I doubt he even knows about Aubree's promotion.

"Yeah, I know. Crazy, huh?"

"I'm not sure if I should be happy for you or pissed off, quite frankly."

I shrug. "Same, dude."

This is how things go in hockey. You grow close with a group of guys, and it seems like nothing could shake that. But then you blink, and someone's getting traded, or someone's hurt and can't play, or someone's retiring from hockey altogether. It's just the nature of the game.

"What did Aubree say?"

I sit on the edge of my bed, my gaze still glued to the TV screen. "I wouldn't know. We broke up yesterday."

"What? What the hell happened? You guys seemed so solid."

I grab the remote to turn off the TV and begin pacing my room. The weight of her betrayal stings all over again, as though I'm still standing in that office hallway, watching her boss shoot me a pitying look.

"It just . . . didn't work out." I force out the words.

"Fuck. Hey. I'm sorry. Do you want me to come over? Or we could meet up and grab a beer?"

I glance at the clock. "It's ten in the morning." I shake my head. "And, no, it's . . . well, it's not *fine*, but it is what it is."

He scoffs. "I'm coming over. You want coffee or what?"

I hesitate, then decide it's easier to just give in. "Yeah. Sure. Thanks, man."

While I wait for Owen to arrive, I glance at my

phone. Aubree's been texting me since yesterday. I haven't replied to any of them. But I scroll through the dozen or so texts again.

Landon, can we talk?

I'm not taking the promotion. I told David to offer it to someone else. I'm not going.

I know you're hurt, and I'm so sorry. This is my fault, but will you please talk to me?

Did you see my message? I'm not going to Vancouver.

Well, *I* am. After that sour thought, I keep scrolling.

Are you there? I really want to talk this through.

Please don't shut me out. I know I messed up. And I'm truly sorry.

Are you okay?

And the hardest one of all to read?

I miss you.

Fuck. Reading those words is like getting kicked in the balls with a hockey skate. I ignore the sharp, painful sting in my chest and delete all the messages without replying.

Thirty minutes later, I've gotten dressed and ordered a new phone online by the time Owen buzzes my apartment. I buzz him in, and a few minutes later, my front door is opening.

"Hey, hey," he says, carrying two large coffees and a greasy brown paper bag.

"Thanks," I say, accepting one of the coffees. "What's that?" I nod toward the bag as my stomach starts to growl. I missed lunch yesterday. And dinner. Because I was too busy sulking and drowning my bad mood in whiskey.

"Oh, dude, tell me you've never been to Tito's before? Their breakfast sandwiches are the best in the city." He reaches into the bag and hands me a foil-wrapped sandwich.

"Never been there, but thanks."

He nods and unwraps his own sandwich. "I still

had so much to teach you about Seattle, and now you're moving on."

"I know. Crazy, right?"

We eat in silence for a few minutes. He was right; this is the best breakfast sandwich I've ever had. Too bad that's still not enough to make up for my sour mood.

When Owen's done, he wipes his hands on a paper napkin and throws his trash inside the bag. Then he leans back against my couch with a sigh. "So, let's talk this out. You and Aubree . . . I thought you were happy."

"I was."

His dark brows pull together. "So, tell me what happened."

"She got promoted at work."

He gives me a confused look. "Okay, so that's generally a good thing, right?"

"It is, except for when she hid it from me for the past two months, and her new job is in, well . . ." I chuckle dryly. "Vancouver, of all places."

He makes a low sound. "Well, if that's not a sign from above, I don't know what is."

"It's not a sign, Owen."

"The hell it's not." He scoffs. "It's fate, dude."

I roll my eyes.

After a few minutes of silence, Owen lets out a long sigh. "Seriously, why is it so hard for hockey players to admit they have feelings?"

Setting down the cup of coffee, I give him an annoyed look. "I admit it, okay? I caught feelings. Big fucking deal. You happy?"

"Not really. Because you're clearly miserable right now, dude."

I shrug but don't deny it, because he's right. This whole thing has me shook. "Yeah, but . . . there's nothing I can do about that now. Aubree is the one who lied to me, not the other way around."

Which means she should be the one to fix it. Only I have no idea how she can fix this. Because, *fuck*.

"Take a deep breath for me," Owen says, his grayish-blue eyes narrowed on mine are filled with real concern.

I release a slow exhale and force a grin onto my face. "Better?"

He rolls his eyes. "Not really. I'm gonna call the guys. We need to take you out, get you drunk."

Maybe this is how dudes handle breakups, I have no idea, since I've never been close enough with a woman for it to hurt when it ended. But this empty feeling inside my chest, I'm guessing this is what getting your fucking heart broken feels like. *Good times.*

He scratches at the stubble on his neck. "So, wait, you guys finally played *bury the salami*, right?"

I crook one eyebrow. "I thought it was called *hide the salami*."

He shrugs. "Just answer the fucking question. Did your salami get some lovin'?"

I chuckle. "No comment."

"Rookie," he deadpans, unamused.

I forgot he wasn't standing on the villa patio listening to me and Aubree that morning after his wedding like everyone else. But I guess as the groom, Owen had bigger things to worry about than the status of my virginity.

"Fine." My mouth lifts in a crooked grin despite my shitty mood, because there's no denying things in the bedroom with Aubree were A-fucking-plus.

"Damn. About time, dude." He reaches his fist out to bump against mine. "So, how was it?"

There aren't words for how I feel about that night with Aubree. Our first time was . . . off-the-charts incredible.

Owen chuckles, reading my silence for exactly what it is. Speechlessness. "That good, huh?"

"Better," I murmur, letting out a sigh.

"Just call her. Talk to her then."

I shake my head. "Be real. The whole thing was doomed from the start. I'm the only idiot who thought it could work."

"Yeah, maybe," he says on an exhale. "But I saw how the two of you were together."

"Yeah? And how were we together?" I say bitterly.

"Well, for starters, you were in love."

I shove the rest of my uneaten food into the bag and carry it into the kitchen. I have no idea what to say to that.

Am I in love with Aubree? Maybe. Probably.

But it doesn't matter. Not anymore.

Just tell that to the achy feeling in the center of my chest—which can go away anytime now.

"You think Becca and I never got in a fight?" He follows me into the kitchen. "Of course we have."

I meet his eyes, leaning one hip against the counter. Something tells me he's not worried about whether his relationship with Becca can survive a trip to Ikea. Sometimes mine has felt that touch and go.

"This is your first fight as a married couple. I'm sure you'll have many more, but now it's up to you to figure out how you want to move forward."

Shaking my head, I draw a deep breath. "We're not moving forward, dude. I'm moving to Canada to play hockey, and she's . . . well, I don't know what she's doing. Her texts say she gave up the promotion, but I really don't care. She wasn't honest with me. Our trust has been broken. Trust is everything. You know that."

Owen gives me a disappointed look. "Couples get in disagreements all the time. It doesn't have to be the end of things. And I'm sure she had her reasons. Just think about it, Covey."

"I've been doing nothing but thinking about it for the past . . ." I look down at my watch. "Twenty-four hours."

"Come on." Owen groans. "I know you're stubborn, but even you've got to see the cosmic significance of you both getting placed in the exact same city. It's meant to be."

I shake my head. "Not seeing it. And really, Parrish, *cosmic significance*? *Meant to be*?"

"Drink that, would ya?" He tips his chin toward my coffee. "You're a cranky bastard when you haven't had your caffeine."

Rolling my eyes at him, I take a sip of my coffee. "Since you're in the mood to dole out advice, help me out here. How did you win over Becca?"

Owen's eyes darken. Without even hesitating, he says, "Easy. I showed her my dick."

"Be serious, jackass."

"I am," Owen says. His expression is solemn, and somehow I fear he might be telling the truth.

"Well, she's seen my dick and she seemed to enjoy it," I mutter, and Owen laughs.

He checks his phone and nods toward the door.

"Hey, I've gotta get going. But, seriously, man, talk to her. Fix this."

I roll my eyes again, taking another sip of coffee as Owen heads for the door. I can't just fix this. How does he not see that?

"And stop sending me pictures from Greece," I call out after him. "If I wanted to see it, I'd fucking go there!"

"Cranky bastard," he calls back just before the door closes.

But once he's gone, I can't stop his words from ringing through my head. As I drop onto my couch and force down the coffee, I start to think that maybe Owen's right. Maybe if my dad had stayed and fought for his relationships, if he hadn't just given in at the first sign of trouble and fled, everything could have been different for him.

I guess I have a decision to make.

Am I going to walk away?

Or am I going to stay and fight for my wife?

Then again, calling Aubree my wife is way too generous. She's never felt like mine, so no matter what Owen has said about *love* or *fate*, I don't know if there's anything left of our relationship to salvage. And that definitely hurts worse than getting kicked in the balls.

I grab my busted phone from the counter, dial the familiar number, and wait for the call to connect.

"Dad," I say once he answers.

"Landon. What's up, son? It's good to hear from you."

I swallow my pride and let out a slow exhale. "I need to talk to you about something."

CHAPTER TWENTY

Vancouver or Bust

Aubree

I f I've learned anything from fifteen years of failed relationships, it's how to mend a broken heart. I've mastered my own personal recipe for recovery—one part tears, two parts junk food, add a sprinkle of vodka-fueled rebounds as needed. Let heal for one to two months, and voilà, I'm back on my feet again.

But when I was driving to my apartment yesterday, desperately trying to blink away my tears to get a clear view of the road, I knew that this would be no ordinary heartbreak. This is the kind of thing I might never recover from. And my night of nonstop crying, hyperventilating, and blowing up Landon's phone with texts only reinforced that fact.

After maybe a grand total of two hours of sleep, the view from my couch this morning is equally bleak. I'm not sure which is less healthy—my breakfast of double-chocolate brownie ice cream that I'm eating straight from the pint, or the fact that my puffy red eyes have been glued to my phone all morning, in hopes of getting a reply from Landon.

Spooning up a heaping bite of ice cream, I catch a glimpse of the light dancing off my wedding ring. I know I shouldn't be wearing it, based on the way Landon all but slammed the door in my face yesterday. But I just can't bring myself to take it off.

I raise the spoon of chocolaty goodness to my lips, hardly tasting the ice cream before swallowing it. I'm not even enjoying it at this point. I'm just trying to numb the pain of the past twenty-four hours.

I've lost my husband, turned down my promotion in hopes of getting him back, and still, he's completely ignoring me. The only thing that hurts more than this complete and utter mess is knowing that it's all my fault. I have no one to blame but myself.

When I go in for my next bite, my spoon hits the bottom of the pint. *Shit*. It's over before I even realized it. Kind of like my marriage. What a depressing thought.

I set the empty carton aside, turning my attention back to the TV. The news is showing some press conference footage from the day before. My gaze ventures to the bottom of the screen, tracking along with the rest of the day's headlines. Some NHL trades are happening, and while they're mostly names I don't recognize, I lean in closer. And then, in a big bold font, streams a string of words that I swear I must be misreading.

BREAKING: LANDON COVINGTON TRADED TO VANCOUVER REBELS, SOURCES SAY.

My heart boomerangs up into my throat, then down to the pit of my stomach. Sources? What sources?

I scramble for my phone, typing Landon's name and the word *Vancouver* into the search bar. Half a dozen articles flood the results, each one echoing the same sentiment. The Ice Hawks are trading their rookie, and the team that wants him happens to be in the city I just turned down a promotion in.

What are the freaking odds?

Was this the thing he wanted to talk to me about yesterday? Yesterday when he came to my office and things disastrously broke right before my eyes?

Frantically, I grab my phone to shoot Landon a message about this, but after one look at the huge string of unanswered texts I sent him last night and I stop dead in my tracks.

Slow your roll, Aubree. If he hasn't texted you back yet, he's not going to respond now.

My thumb hovers briefly over the call button, but then I close out of my contacts altogether and open my email instead. There's a new message from David Stone, his response to my email turning down the promotion last night.

Aubree, I'm sorry to hear that you're declining the position. Please take the weekend to reconsider, and we'll move forward on Monday morning.

My eyes lock on those last two words. Monday morning. Less than forty-eight hours from now. Which means I have no time to waste.

I toss my phone down, leap up from the couch, and race toward my bathroom with a renewed sense of hope. Because if I don't have hope, I have nothing right now.

I hop in the shower, run a razor over my legs, and scrub the depression out of my pores with a generous amount of apricot body wash. Once I'm toweled off, I dig through my closet, emerging with the navy-blue T-shirt dress I wore that first morning in Vegas. After a few coats of mascara, a swipe of lip gloss, and a quick pep talk in my bathroom mirror, I'm out the door and into the driver's seat of my SUV.

The new-car smell is still thick in the air. I've hardly put ten miles on this car, opting instead to use my old trusty sedan for the past week, but it feels right to drive it today. And I guess if he turns me away, I can give him the keys back and find a way home.

As I press the button for the ignition, I shake off that depressing thought and focus on the task at hand—getting to Landon as fast as I possibly can.

I zoom through town, well over the speed limit, and by some miracle, make it to Landon's apartment without getting pulled over. I take it as a sign from the universe that I'm doing the right thing by having this conversation with him in person.

My strappy sandals carry me through the parking garage and to the doors of the elevator, which open to welcome me in. I scan the access card he gave me and hit the button for the top floor, and when the elevator shifts into motion, my stomach lurches with it. It's not until the doors are opening again that I realize I haven't decided on exactly what to say to him.

Too late now. Here goes everything.

Approaching his door, I lift one shaky hand to knock. But to my surprise, before my knuckles can make contact, the door swings open on a totally unsuspecting Landon, who just barely catches himself from walking straight into me. He blinks at me with wide, startled eyes, frozen in the doorway with keys in hand, one arm already shrugging on his favorite leather jacket.

"Aubree." My name falls off his lips like a soft, desperate prayer, sending goose bumps scampering down my limbs. "What are you doing here?"

I draw in a shaky breath, my throat threatening to close up. *What am I doing here? Groveling?* I don't want to admit that. Instead, I blurt out the first thing that comes to mind.

"I saw that you're being transferred to Vancouver."

His brows push together with skepticism. "You were watching the sports channel? You know they don't play *Annie* on there, right?"

I purse my lips, holding back an unexpected laugh. Leave it to Landon to make me laugh when I feel so awful. But the fact that he's joking with me is a good sign. I was half expecting him to breeze past me, ignoring me in person just like he did over text.

"Were you on your way to sign with the Rebels?" I nod toward the keys in his hand, and he looks down at them too, spinning the key ring around in his nimble fingers.

For a moment, I'm worried he's going to turn around and lock me out. But instead, he looks up at me, the slightest hint of a smile threatening the corners of his lips.

"Actually, I was on my way to you."

I blink up at him in disbelief. "Really?"

"Really." His brilliant blue eyes flicker with something familiar. Hope, I think. Or maybe it's fear. "I've felt like shit since you left yesterday."

My heart swells as he reaches out to grab my

trembling hand, running his thumb along the band of my wedding ring.

"That's why I'm here too. We need to talk," I say.

He nods. "We do. Are you okay?"

Emotion rising in my throat, I shake my head.

"Come here," he says softly, opening his arms.

I step into them, pressing my face into the front of his shirt and inhale. The distinct scent of musk and male and Landon arrests me. How in the world did I think I could live without this smell? Without this man? And for what? A promotion? A job? No way. I'm his. I never planned to be, but there's no denying it now.

Lifting my face toward his, I smile weakly. "Thanks. I needed that."

He shifts, putting some distance between us yet again. "I was wifeless for less than twenty-four hours," he says, his voice as serious as I've ever heard it, "and it was fucking awful. But it took losing you for me to realize a few really important things."

I lift a brow. "Like what?"

"Like I never want to let you go again. And . . ." His Adam's apple bobs as his gaze drops to his feet momentarily, then back up to meet with mine. "I guess I should let you say what you came here to say." He takes a step back, and a cloud of worry crosses his features.

After a quiet moment, I work up enough courage to respond, my tone a little shaky. "I'm sorry for everything. I just . . . I didn't think I could actually do this. Didn't think I could rely on another person when it could all go up in smoke."

He touches my cheek with his thumb. "I know. But I'm going to be there. Today. Tomorrow. When shit goes south. During the good times, the bad, and everything in between."

My throat tightens, and I inhale slowly. "It killed me that I hurt you yesterday. I went home and sobbed like I haven't since my dog, Lucy, died when I was thirteen. It felt like the death of something real, you know? Something life changing and so important to me was poof. Gone. It killed me." I take a shuddering inhale and continue. "And me and you . . . it's crazy how it all started, but what we have is real. I see that now, and I believe in it. In us."

He nods, still watching me with a tender expression.

"What we have isn't something I'm just going to give up on," I say, gathering courage. "Our relationship is bigger than where we live, or what job we have, or who's getting transferred where."

Landon's eyes darken as they lock onto mine, his expression filled with so much emotion, I could burst. "I love you, Aubree. I love you, and I never want to be apart again."

My breath catches, and I have to hold tight to his hand to keep the shock of the moment from knocking me over. That look in his eyes—it wasn't hope or fear. It was something way better.

It was love.

I squeeze his hand extra tight. "I love you too, Landon." The words sound so natural, but they leave my lips tingling because they're the absolute truth. "More than I've loved anyone before."

When his hand finds the small of my back, tugging me in for a soft, delicate kiss, the tingling spreads to every inch of my body. And, God, it feels like heaven. I find my grip on his shoulders as I press up to my tiptoes, deepening our kiss. When he finally pulls back, I'm able to take in my first full breath since yesterday.

That realization is followed by a huge sense of relief.

I haven't broken everything. Landon loves me.

"So, Vancouver, huh?" I ask, steadying myself against him.

"Vancouver." He gives me a firm nod, his expression tightening in a moment of seriousness. "I hope you didn't mean what you said in your texts about telling David you didn't want the job."

I smirk, squeezing his side playfully. "Oh, so you did read my texts."

He rolls his eyes, feigning annoyance, but his smile gives him away. "Let's forget about your bombardment of texts for now. What did you tell David?"

"I tried to reject the offer, but he told me we'd discuss it Monday after I took the weekend to think about it."

"And have you thought about it?"

I nod. "A lot."

"And?"

"And I want to be where you are, so if you're staying here, so am I. And if you're going, I guess

I'm moving to Canada too."

An enormous smile breaks out on his face, bringing out that dimple I love so much. I press my thumb against it, which only makes him smile wider.

"And if I got transferred to Minnesota?" he asks with a smirk.

"Then I'd buy some warm mittens. You're not going to scare me away, mister."

"I hope you know you're moving in with me," he says. "I refuse to spend another night without my wife."

"I kind of like it when you're bossy." I grin. "But, yeah, I think I'm down for living together. I like the idea of having my husband whenever I want."

It's quiet for a moment, not that I mind. I'm all too happy to be getting lost in his eyes.

"So, what now?" he finally asks.

I chew my lower lip for a second before deciding. "Now you get your heinie back into your apartment."

He cringes at my use of his least favorite word.

"Yeah? What for?"

I slide my thumbs through his belt loops, gazing up at him with mischievous eyes. "For make-up sex. *Duh*."

Landon's dimple reappears, his face breaking into an enormous smile as he slips the key into the door. "That's another first for me."

"I like being your first," I say, chewing on my lip. "And I just might be your last, if I'm lucky."

"I think I'm the lucky one." He nods toward my wedding ring, then pushes the door open, waving me inside. "Now, come on. We've got some making up to do."

CHAPTER TWENTY-ONE

Old Friends and New Beginnings

Aubree

"**G**ood morning, sunshine." Elise yawns, rolling out her yoga mat next to mine.

The clock on the wall says 8:50, just ten minutes before the start of my favorite Saturday morning yoga class. The gang is officially all here, dressed in leggings and tank tops, and ready to get their flow on.

"Morning!" Ana wiggles her fingers toward Elise in a tiny wave, then presses into downward dog, pedaling her feet to stretch out her calves.

The two of us arrived early, as usual, to have enough time to stretch out and chat before the rest of the girls began filtering in, grabbing mats to set up next to us near the back of the studio. Thank God for Ana. She's been a consistent yoga buddy for me these past few years, even when the other girls had absolutely zero interest in tagging along.

"How are you guys this flexible this early in the morning?" Elise eyes Ana's form suspiciously while trying, and failing, to touch her toes.

Much like most of my friends, Elise has never been one for yoga. Which is why it's so special that they're all here this morning. When I messaged the group chat with the idea of us all going to class together, I was expecting pushback and pleas for brunch. Instead, everyone agreed to be at the studio bright and early.

Half of September has slipped away, and we're just two weeks away from the big move to Vancouver, so everyone has been especially insistent on seeing plenty of one another before I go.

"So, what's new with you guys?" I ask, working my legs into lotus pose.

Becca pipes up from behind me, where she's barely managing a quadricep stretch. Ignoring my question, she asks about me instead. "Are you and Landon all ready for the move?"

"As ready as we can be," I say on a sigh. "I feel like my whole life is in cardboard boxes. Meanwhile, I don't think my husband has even thought about packing."

Everyone chuckles, except Sara, who looks a little rattled. "Confession time . . . I'm still not used to you calling him your husband."

"Honestly, me either." I laugh. "Probably because we skipped over the whole boyfriend-and-girlfriend part."

"And the fiancée part," Elise says, wiggling her ring finger in our direction. She hasn't missed an opportunity to show off that diamond since Justin put it on her finger.

"Yeah, Bree, you skipped the fun stuff." Ana comes down from her downward dog, pretzeling her legs beneath her. "We didn't get to throw you an engagement party or anything."

"We could do one now," Bailey says. "A delayed engagement slash wedding slash going-away celebration."

The girls break out into excited chatter, talking over one another in three simultaneous conversations about decorations, food, and drinks. It takes a few glares from other women in the studio, who are desperately trying to find their Zen, for everyone to notice their sudden volume increase.

"Shh, guys," I hiss through my teeth, motioning for everyone to bring it down a few notches. "I don't need a big party or anything. Landon and I are already planning on going on a delayed honeymoon next summer. That's all the celebration I need."

"Okay, but *we* don't get to go on the honeymoon," Becca says in a hushed, yet sassy voice. "We want to celebrate you too. Plus, it's an excuse for everyone to get together before you leave."

I mull it over, chewing my lower lip in thought. She makes a good point. "How about I ask Landon and see what he thinks?"

"He'll say yes as long as it's something you want to do," Elise says, her tone pleading.

"Come on, let us do this. We'll keep it casual, I promise." Ana blinks at me with big puppy-dog eyes.

God, these girls make it impossible to say no.

"Fine. Go for it," I say, raising my palms in surrender. "But nothing fancy. Let's keep it low-key and casual, okay?"

Soft, soothing music starts to play, which is our cue to quit talking and get our meditation on. Something my party-planning friends make it nearly impossible to achieve. Throughout the whole class, I can hear Ana and Bailey whispering to each other, discussing dates and locations.

The second class is over, Bailey scrambles to her locker to grab her phone, texting Landon to confirm the details. Next Friday, seven p.m., Landon's apartment. They'll all come over at five to decorate, meaning it looks like the hubby and I are going out to dinner beforehand.

I roll my eyes, sliding my shoes back on before heading for the door. "You guys are insane, you know that?"

"Nope," Ana says with an enormous grin. "We just love you, that's all."

• • •

It's just past seven when Landon and I step out of the elevator and toward his apartment, where we can already hear the party underway. It's Friday night, and we're fresh off a sushi dinner and a mini make-out sesh in the parking garage, ready to celebrate the crazy past few months the two of us have had with a low-key gathering of our friends.

At least, that's what I told my friends I wanted.

But by the sounds of clinking glasses and ambient music spilling out from behind Landon's apartment door, I somehow get the feeling tonight's party isn't going to be as chill as I anticipated.

"Do you think I have to knock at my own apartment?" Landon asks, his dark brows knitting together as he digs in his pocket for his keys.

I lift a shoulder, weaving my fingers into the spaces between his. "They probably wouldn't even hear you over the music."

We decide to just walk in, finding the door unlocked. Inside, we're greeted by a dozen friendly faces, a few of them unexpected. I knew we'd have all the regulars, but it looks like Ana's hot-tempered boyfriend, Jason, turned up for the party, along with Grant and Jordie, who I haven't seen since the wedding. When Becca said that this party would be a good way to get everyone together, she really meant *everyone*. As much as I put up a fight about it, I really am grateful to have all my favorite people together one last time before we leave.

"Hey, hey! Right on time," Owen calls from the kitchen, lifting two beer bottles in the air so as not to spill them as he weaves through the crowd.

Landon's apartment is spacious, but it's still a

one-bedroom, not really designed to hold two dozen people. Becca follows a few steps behind Owen, and pulls me in for a big hug.

"Welcome to the first, and therefore *best*, engagement slash wedding slash going-away party you've ever been to." She gestures to the sparkly silver banner above the couch that reads CONGRATULATIONS! and another right below it that reads BON VOYAGE.

"For some reason, the party store didn't sell any combination wedding and going-away party banners." Bailey emerges from the crowded kitchen and hands me a flute of champagne.

"This is too much," I say, gasping as I take in the black and silver balloons dotting the corners of the room, along with the twinkle lights draped along the granite countertops. It feels like New Year's Eve in September, in the best possible way.

"Just wait till you see the games!" Ana pulls me into the living room, showing off the trivia game she's made out of a poster board. She's written MARRIAGE BOOT CAMP 101 in big bold letters across the top, and each colorful square has a different question written on it, meant to test how well couples know each other.

Apparently, when I said tonight should be low-key and casual, what Ana heard was *annoying party games*, the kind you play at a baby shower or bridal party. Yes, because I'm sure my new husband is going to love answering trivia questions and diapering a baby doll. Except Landon's smile hasn't faded once, and his rich laughter floats across the room to me even now.

God, I'm so lucky to have him.

Once everyone has a drink and a plate of appetizers, we congregate in the living room, pairing off into couples to play the game. Jordie and Grant, the only single guys here, are good sports about being a "Bro Power Couple," insisting that they'll beat all the actual couples, which gets a good laugh.

"Come here, Jason." Ana waves over her boyfriend, who has been sitting on the couch scrolling through his phone since we got here. "We're starting the game."

Reluctantly, Jason pockets his phone and stalks over to where Ana's seated on the carpet, divvying out poker chips to use as game pieces and explaining the rules—roll the dice, move your poker chip that many spaces, and answer the question you land on about your significant other. Clearly, she put a lot of work into this. Honestly, my heart could burst, no matter how cheesy it is.

"The guests of honor get to go first," Ana says, handing off the dice to Landon.

He rolls them on the board, moves the chip along, and lands on a square marked FAVORITE MOVIE.

"Piece of cake," he says, shooting me a knowing grin. "*Annie.*"

I nod enthusiastically. "Got it. And yours is *Shawshank Redemption.*"

"Yup."

We high-five, both of us beaming with pride. Not bad for a couple that's only been together for three months.

"Us next!" Becca giddily snatches up the dice, giving them a roll. She and Owen ace the question about favorite sports teams, which seems unfair seeing as they both say the Seattle Ice Hawks.

After a few more couples ace their questions, including Jordie and Grant, Ana and Jason are up.

"You know this one," Ana says, clapping her hands between words for emphasis. "My favorite animal! It's easy!"

Her boyfriend has *clueless* written all over his face. "I don't know it. Can I just guess?"

She lets out an exasperated huff, turning toward the group. "Can I give him a clue?"

"Go for it." Asher shrugs. "You made the game."

"When we went to the pumpkin patch and they had that petting zoo . . ." She nods toward him, waiting for him to fill in the blanks. "Remember? There was one animal I really, really wanted to pet? Even though there were tons of little kids in line?"

Jason stares at her blankly. "Dog?"

"Oh my God." She rolls her eyes, throwing her hands up with a frustrated groan. "It's a goat. Specifically, I love baby goats. You totally knew that."

"Well, sorry I haven't memorized every damn thing about you, Ana." Jason's jaw tics, his dark eyes narrowing to a squint. "Not every word out of your mouth is fucking gold, you know."

"Cool it, dude," Landon says in a low voice, giving Jason a nudge. "It's just a game."

"Whatever. This is fucking stupid," Jason says on a sigh.

Ana shoots her boyfriend a pleading look. "Can we take it easy on the f-bombs tonight and just relax?" She reaches out to rest a hand on his shoulder, but he shrugs out of her reach.

"Don't fucking tell me to relax." He pushes to his feet, stepping over the game board and toward the door. "I'll catch you guys later."

And just like that, he's gone, leaving his teary-eyed girlfriend on the floor, confused and hurt.

For a stunned moment, everyone is quiet. The only sound is the ventilation system kicking on and a soft whoosh of air. Ana looks stunned, shaken, and my heart aches for her.

"I . . . I . . ." Ana stammers, her gaze darting between me and the door. "I'm so sorry. I think maybe I should just go."

"You don't have to leave, Ana," I say, giving her a pleading look.

"I know, but I just . . ." She shakes her head. I can tell she's about three minutes away from real tears.

Crap. I remember being in that situation at the brunch table in Vegas. All I wanted was to run away before my friends saw me cry.

"Whatever you want to do," I say. "It's up to you."

"I think it's better if I just go," she says quietly.

"I can take you," Grant says, rising and holding out a hand to help Ana to her feet. "As much as Jordie and I are a power couple at this game, I'd better quit while I'm ahead."

Something inside me squeezes at the sight of this huge, hulking man of few words and even fewer emotions offering to be her savior for the night.

Then again, I recall the way Grant's jaw muscles flexed when Jason verbally sparred with Ana in the kitchen earlier. It was like he was grinding his molars to avoid getting between them. And while I've never seen him offer to drive someone home before, you'd have to be blind not to notice the way Grant sometimes looks at Ana. Then again, how could you not look at Ana in any way but with fondness? She's adorable and tiny. And sweet, like one of those little elves who lives in a tree house baking cookies.

Ana wipes a tear from her cheek with the side of her hand, sniffling out a *thank you* before saying her good-byes to everyone, promising me that we'll do yoga again before I go and that she'll text me when she's safe at home.

"Let me know who wins the game," she says with a forced smile as Grant helps her into her coat, then holds the door open for her on their way out.

I have no qualms about them leaving together. From the limited time I've spent with him, I know Grant is a good guy. Unlike Jason, apparently.

Sara clears her throat, breaking the painful silence in the room. "Um, do you guys still want to play the game?"

"Let's just move on," Bailey says. "Since Jordie is flying solo now."

We all agree to call it a tie on the trivia game and opt for the game Becca planned, which involves diapering baby dolls. It feels a bit more suited for a baby shower than tonight's celebration, but I'm half a glass of champagne in, so I can't be bothered to ask too many questions.

I proudly claim the gold medal as the fastest person to diaper the stiff baby doll, but Asher's years of practice as an uncle gets him the most diapers taken off and put on in a minute. Meanwhile, Landon can hardly figure out how to open the diaper packaging.

"I didn't think it was possible to be that bad at this, babe." I laugh, cringing as my husband literally puts the doll's head through one of the leg holes.

"This is hard." He groans, handing the doll over to me. "Can you do it?"

"No way." I down the rest of the glass of champagne, shaking my head. "You'll need the practice if we're ever going to have one of these for real."

"Speaking of which, I made something for you guys," Bailey says, frantically thumbing through the photos on her phone. When she lands on what she's looking for, she pushes a button and projects onto the screen an image with baby pictures of the both of us, and the words CONGRATS, LANDON AND AUBREE! in big, curly letters.

My eyes gloss over the familiar shot of me in my stroller, my dark curls tumbling out of my winter hat. I'm a bit more concerned with the oversize child who, despite being bald, looks like he weighs the same as a toddler.

"Oh my God, Landon, you were a giant baby!" Elise squawks.

"Well, procreating is out of the question." I laugh, only half sarcastic. No way am I pushing anything the size of *that* out of my lady parts.

"I wasn't that big," Landon says. "Ten or eleven pounds tops, when I was born."

My eyes widen. "Are you kidding me? Huh-uh. No way."

Landon waves off my comment. "Oh, come on. We both know you want kids."

"I did. Past tense. Not anymore." I fold my arms over my chest, nodding toward the humongous infant on the screen. Who is this man's father? The jolly green giant?

"We're going to make pretty babies someday, sweetheart." He kisses my forehead, completely undeterred by the fact that I'm still gawking at the screen.

"I quite like my pelvic floor where it's currently at, thank you very much." I scoff, playfully shoving him off me.

"I'm going to knock you up, Aubree. Just face it."

I smile, giving his cheek a gentle pat. "No way. We'll adopt."

He chuckles, but then his blue eyes lock with mine. I watch them shift from playful to serious in a split second, and feel the weight of the moment. Despite us being surrounded by our friends, something about this feels like it's just between the two of us. Like we've found this bit of privacy in a crowded room.

God, I love him. This crazy, stubborn, sweet man.

"Whatever you want," he says on an exhale. "But either way, I can't wait to watch you become a mom."

"And that's our cue to go," Owen says, hopping to his feet. He shoots Landon a wink as he corrals the rest of our friends toward the door. "Party's over, you guys. I think somebody's got twenty-three years of sexual repression to make up for."

And make up for it, we will.

But first, Landon pulls me close for a slow, sweet kiss. "I love you, baby."

"And I love you," I murmur, touching the stubble on his cheek.

EPILOGUE

Landon

Six weeks later

"**N**ice try, fucker," Asher says, skating past me and managing to steal the puck like it's effortless for him.

And maybe it is, because as much as I've tried to tell myself that tonight's game is just another game, it's becoming obvious that it's more than that. It's the first time I've seen my old teammates since I got traded to the Vancouver Rebels. And it's only the second time I've skated in my new red jersey. Let's just say I might be feeling the pressure.

I sprint to catch up with him, checking him hard into the corner. "Can't let you make me look like a punk in my own house. Especially not with my wife watching in the stands."

"I'm not going to go easy on you." Asher

grunts, freeing himself from my hold.

"Never asked you to."

I focus my attention on getting down the ice, crossing the blue line as I snap off a pass to my new teammate, Arvi Cedrik, a funny-as-hell guy from Finland. I get into position and he slaps it back to me, and with a one-timer Arvi and I practiced over and over this week, I find Owen's five-hole, scoring the first point of the night, and my first ever goal as a Rebel.

The Vancouver crowd goes wild, and the air horn gives a sharp blast.

Fuck yeah.

I can't deny how good that felt. My team surrounds me, thumping me on the back and helmet in congratulations.

"I'm going to kick your ass for that, Covey!" Owen shouts over to me.

"Keep dreaming, Parrish!" I call back, grinning like an idiot.

Just as play gets back underway, I'm checked hard into the wall by Jordie. "Hey, fucker, how's Canada?"

"Cold," I say with a laugh. I'm still grinning as I make my way down the ice.

"Red looks terrible on you," Asher says at the next face-off.

Teddy nods his agreement. "Awful."

"I don't know," I say with a chuckle. "I've been told I pull it off."

Next up, Grant slams into me with the force of a semi truck. "We're not friends on the ice anymore, rookie. But it's fucking good to see you owning the ice up here."

"I was taught by the best."

He shakes his head before stealing the puck from me and skating toward Justin.

Bastard.

A minute later, I skate back to the bench, ready to give our second line a shift and to catch my breath. When I step over the wall, my gaze finds Aubree in the stands. She's smiling huge and chatting with Arvi's wife and their six-year-old son.

That's when everything becomes crystal clear to me.

It doesn't matter what color jersey I'm wearing, or what team I'm playing on, or where I'm living, because wherever Aubree is, that will always be my home. And just because they're not my teammates anymore doesn't make these guys any less my friends. It's hard to wipe the smile from my face after that.

After the game and a quick shower, I give an interview to the waiting media before rushing to my car. I haven't been able to stop smiling, and I'm feeling really damn good about our win tonight.

After climbing into my car, I dial Aubree.

"Hey, baby," I say as soon as she answers.

She squeals into the phone. "I'm so freaking proud of you!"

I laugh and wave at the security guard Len as I pull out of the arena's parking garage and then out onto the streets of Vancouver. "I'm not going to lie, that goal in the first felt really fucking good."

"You're incredible, babe," she says, her voice soft and sultry. "I can't wait for you to get home, because I have a surprise for you."

As if I needed any more incentive to get home. "Be there in ten."

We'd looked into buying a house in the suburbs

where a couple of my married teammates live, but ended up buying a condo in the heart of the city instead. It's only a ten-minute drive to the arena, fifteen from our training facility, and Aubree can walk to her office from our building.

Plus, since I travel so much during the season and have to leave Aubree for chunks of time, I like the extra security we have at our building with the doorman, and secure access to our floor. Knowing she'll be safe when I'm not home makes it a tiny bit easier to leave for away games.

Our place isn't extravagant, but we have two bedrooms, so if and when our family of two expands, we have the space. And it's something we've been talking about more lately.

When I arrive home, I toss my bag onto the entryway floor and go off in search of Aubree. "Bree?"

There's a lamp on in the living room, but otherwise the only light is courtesy of the city itself— twinkling headlights on the cars zipping down Highway 1A in the distance, and glittering lights from the nearby high-rises. It's a pretty city, and I haven't tired of the view.

"I'm starving, babe. Where are you?" I call out.

"Back here. In the bedroom," she says.

I turn down the hall just as Aubree emerges from the master bedroom. She's dressed in a pair of gray boxer shorts, tall fuzzy socks, and a red Rebels sweatshirt.

"Sorry, I wanted to get comfortable. You made it home quick."

"Absolutely no need to be sorry; you look sexy as hell. Now, get over here. Your husband needs a kiss."

With a giggle, she steps toward me, and I pull her into my chest. She lifts up on her toes to treat me to a warm kiss.

"I'm hungry," I murmur against her mouth. "Is my surprise food? Please say it's food."

She laughs. "I got you a double serving of ramen. You didn't see the takeout bag on the counter?"

"Nope. I focused on finding you."

She shakes her head as her cheeks flush pink. "Come on, let's feed you. But, no, it's not the surprise."

"Hmm, now I'm intrigued." I follow her into

the kitchen, still wondering about what her surprise could be.

"It's a shame the guys were traveling back to Seattle right after the game," she says as I help myself to a pair of chopsticks and dig into a gigantic bite of noodles and broth.

"Yeah, I know. It would have been fun to have them over."

She nods. "Speaking of having people over . . ."

"What?" I give her a questioning look.

"My parents RSVP'd for Thanksgiving. They can come."

I nod. "That's great, right?"

She tilts her chin. "And so did your dad."

"Oh."

"Yup." She laughs.

"So we're doing this? Hosting, I mean?" I say around another mouthful of food.

Shrugging, she steals a shrimp from my steaming bowl of noodles. "It appears so."

"It'll be a good thing," I say, smiling at her.

We've been wanting our families to meet for a while now, and have been trying to find a way to make that happen—while also coordinating an international move, the start of the hockey season, and Aubree starting a new job. My mom came up to Vancouver the weekend we moved to meet Aubree for the first time and help us unpack. As I expected, she immediately bonded and fell in love with Aubree. I couldn't wait for Dad to meet her in person, although they regularly chat on the phone when he calls.

I finish my dinner while Aubree fills me in on her plan for the Thanksgiving meal. Apparently, she's already recruited Arvi's wife to help her prep, and there's something about needing to order new sheets for the guest room.

"Well, that's some surprise," I say, placing my now-empty takeout container in the trash.

"Babe, that wasn't the surprise." She smiles, her eyes twinkling with happiness.

"It wasn't?"

She scurries out of the kitchen to retrieve an envelope from the coffee table, which she hands me with a huge grin. It's from the Insurance Corporation of British Columbia.

"Okay . . ." I turn the envelope over in my hands.

"Open it!" she says excitedly.

I wander into the living room and Aubree follows, plopping down onto the couch beside me wearing a massive smile.

Inside the envelope, glued to a piece of paper, is Aubree's new Canadian driver's license. It takes me a minute to understand why she's so excited about me seeing her driver's license.

Then I see it, and my heart nearly bursts with happiness.

"Fuck, baby," I murmur, my eyes meeting hers. "But why?"

She smiles and scoots in closer to me. "For you, my husband. I wanted to give you this."

I run my thumb over the letters of her new name. *Aubree Covington*. She changed her name for me. Pride swells within me.

"I thought you weren't going to."

We talked about this. Aubree's an independent woman, and I totally respect that. It was her decision. And now that she's made it, a different one than I was expecting, my heart feels three times the size it did earlier.

"I like the idea of us having the same name." She touches my hand, and I open my palm so she can slide her hand into mine. "I always thought I'd be giving something up by changing my last name, but then I realized I wasn't giving up anything. I was gaining so much in return. Plus, I want to share the same name as the love of my life and the father of my future children. I want us all to have the same name."

"Mrs. Covington," I murmur.

The twinkle in her eyes beams bright. "Are you happy?"

"This is the best surprise ever," I say, leaning over to kiss her.

I'm just so damn happy she chose to do this. I can't believe we're *the Covingtons*. It sounds so official. My brain starts spinning with all kinds of things guys probably aren't supposed to think about, like monogrammed towels and matching luggage.

Aubree leans in too, planting her hand on my chest, and treats me to a slow, sweet kiss. "Do you know why I love you?"

"Because of my ability to make you orgasm with my tongue, my fingers, and my cock?"

She laughs, shaking her head. "Impressive, but no. I love you because you've always accepted me just as I am. You let me be me, and figure all this out in my own time."

I nod, touching her cheek. "We're in this together. I knew you were going to be my forever from the moment I met you. There's just one problem," I growl.

"What's that?" she whispers.

"I think your surprise had an unintended consequence." My gaze drops to my lap, and Aubree's follows. "I suddenly feel really fucking horny." I feel slightly territorial too, but she doesn't need to know that part.

One of her eyebrows lifts in a challenging smirk. "My driver's license made you horny?"

"Very."

She crawls from her spot next to me and into my lap. "Then I might be able to do something about that." With a sultry look, my wife kisses me. And it's the perfect kiss. Slow and hot and wet.

"Shit." I shift her in my lap.

Aubree meets my eyes with a look of concern. "What is it?"

"Just let me brush my teeth first." All I can think about is the fact that I just ate, and my breath is probably terrible.

She laughs but motions for me to go ahead. "If you must."

Hoisting myself up from the couch, I adjust the front of my pants and head for the master bath. At the sink, I grab my toothbrush and get to work, trying not to laugh at the fact that my Fleshlight is resting on a hand towel on the counter where I left it after washing it.

We rarely use the toy anymore, but last night, Aubree was feeling frisky and asked if she could use it on me. Which led to her stroking it up and down my shaft with a ton of lube, which led to me begging her to stop and ride me instead, which then led to the hottest sex ever.

My pulse spikes at the memory. My wife is better than your wife—FYI.

I finish brushing and rinse my mouth. One last quick glance in the mirror makes me smile, because the light catches the platinum of my wedding band. Even though I've been wearing my ring every day since Aubree surprised me with it, I haven't gotten tired of seeing it on my hand. I don't think I ever will.

"Lovey," Aubree calls from the living room, sounding impatient.

I smile and call back, "Coming, babe."

I've got a hot date on the couch with my wife, the woman of my dreams. Life doesn't get any better than that.

• • •

I hope you enjoyed *Down and Dirty*! Up next is Grant and Ana's story in *Wild for You.*

WILD FOR YOU

He's growly. Grumpy. Stubborn.

And now, my new roommate.

Walking away from my disastrous last relationship was an easy decision, but moving in with a friend-of-a-friend hockey star who's rarely home? Not quite as simple, because Grant makes me feel things even I don't understand.

One thing's for certain, though. I definitely shouldn't have crawled into his bed that night.

• • •

There's a brightness to her eyes I can't seem to look away from.

She's beautiful. Smart. Tempting.

And a little fragile.

I've never been anyone's knight in shining armor, but when Ana needed a place to stay, it was easy to move her in with me. Not so simple, though, is keeping my hands—or my mouth—to myself. And the night she crawls into my bed and shares her body with me has me conjuring up all kinds of ideas about our future.

Until a big surprise I never saw coming changes everything.

ACKNOWLEDGMENTS

A humongous bear hug to my editor Pam Berehulke. You're the best editor in the whole wide world. I can't believe it's been, what . . . five years? Six? Time flies when you're having fun!

To Alyssa Garcia, thank you for putting up with me. I know I'm forgetful and a little crazy, but I want you to know I appreciate the heck out of you, and I'm so thankful we're on this journey together. Rachel Brookes, your enthusiasm for this series and your editorial eye have been so appreciated. I'm grateful for you and your friendship. Thank you to Stacy Garcia for your unending excitement and support of my stories. You always bring a smile to my face.

A heartfelt thank-you to all the readers who have followed this series. I have so enjoyed writing about these tough, yet sweet jocks and the strong women they fall for. I also love hearing which hot jock was your favorite, so please consider leaving a review at the retailer where you purchased the book, and/or joining my reader group, linked on the next page, so I can hear your thoughts!

Get Two Free books

Sign up for my newsletter and I'll automatically send you two free books.

www.kendallryanbooks.com/newsletter

Follow Kendall

Website

www.kendallryanbooks.com

Facebook

www.facebook.com/kendallryanbooks

Twitter

www.twitter.com/kendallryan1

Instagram

www.instagram.com/kendallryan1

Newsletter

www.kendallryanbooks.com/newsletter

About the Author

A *New York Times*, *Wall Street Journal*, and *USA TODAY* bestselling author of more than two dozen titles, Kendall Ryan has sold over two million books, and her books have been translated into several languages in countries around the world. Her books have also appeared on the *New York Times* and *USA TODAY* bestseller list more than three dozen times. Kendall has been featured in publications such as *USA TODAY*, *Newsweek*, and *In Touch Magazine*. She lives in Texas with her husband and two sons.

To be notified of new releases or sales, join Kendall's private Mailing List.

www.kendallryanbooks.com/newsletter

Get even more of the inside scoop when you join Kendall's private Facebook group, Kendall's Kinky Cuties:

www.facebook.com/groups/kendallskinkycuties

Other Books by Kendall Ryan

Unravel Me

Filthy Beautiful Lies Series

The Room Mate

The Play Mate

The House Mate

The Impact of You

Screwed

The Fix Up

Dirty Little Secret

xo, Zach

Baby Daddy

Tempting Little Tease

Bro Code

Love Machine

Flirting with Forever

Dear Jane

Finding Alexei

Boyfriend for Hire

The Two Week Arrangement

Seven Nights of Sin

Playing for Keeps

All the Way

Trying to Score

Crossing the Line

The Bedroom Experiment

For a complete list of Kendall's books, visit:
www.kendallryanbooks.com/all-books/

Printed in Great Britain
by Amazon